*Love and Death, & Other Disasters*

Other books by the author:

*The Sea of Light*
*Shimoni's Lover*
*Snow*
*Water Dancer*

# Love and Death, & Other Disasters

STORIES 1977-1995

## JENIFER LEVIN

Firebrand
Books
Ithaca, New York

Stories in this collection have previously appeared in the following anthologies: *Dyke Fairy Tales* (Richard Kasak), *Heatwave* (Alyson Publications), *Sportsdykes* (St. Martin's Press), *Tasting Life Twice* (Avon), and *Women on Women 3* (Plume/ Penguin); and in the *Global City Review*.

Book and cover design by Nightwood
Cover photograph by Claude Cole

Printed in the United States on acid-free paper by McNaughton & Gunn

10 9 8 7 6 5 4 3 2 1

Library of Congress Cataloging-in-Publication Data

Levin, Jenifer.
    Love and death & other disasters : stories 1977–1995 / Jenifer Levin.
        p.   cm.
    ISBN 1-56341-079-6 (cloth : alk. paper). —ISBN 1-56341-078-8 (paper : alk. paper)
        1. Lesbians—Social life and customs—Fiction. I. Title.
    PS3562.E8896L6   1996
    813'.54—dc20                                                    96-41687
                                                                          CIP

# Contents

# *Preface*

ere's how it was for me: I started writing and attempting to publish some of these stories in the late 1970s. Back then no one would—publish them, I mean—least of all the lesbian and feminist presses. Butch-Femme had nothing to do with lesbianism, I was told; and the sexual style expressed in this fiction was oppressive to women.

You know, feminists get a lot of flack these days, and some of it's well-deserved. But I think I understand now how, in the context of the times twenty years ago, the response to this work wasn't totally unreasonable.

So I forgot about trying to get any short stories published and just kept writing them for myself. Publicly and professionally I turned to the novel, and have had four novels and a lot of nonfiction published by the mainstream press over the past two decades.

It just goes to show you: If you live long enough, you come back into fashion. Now, finally, as we approach the millennium, I've been selling short stories like hotcakes.

When I first began writing about lesbian life, relationships, sexual encounter, and truth as I knew it, I was a young dyke in search of love, newly returned to this country, tortured about being queer. Yes—I was one of those suicidal kids you read about now, in these hipper days of PFLAG, the kind who, as a teen, wrote things in her diary like, "Please, God, don't do it, don't make me homosexual!"

To no avail. From an early age, queerness has been my social and sexual destiny. And today, quite alive, I thank my lucky stars.

I thank all the lesbians who have loved me—and who taught me how to love them, body and soul.

I thank those gay men I danced with every night in the big cities of my youth. They were my first ecstatic bacchanalian healing friends, who taught me how to laugh and how to gain spiritual wisdom from being different in America. Nearly all are gone now. I bless them for their courageous love, reaching out as they did to touch me even from beds of suffering and death.

Most of all, I thank the women in my life—and the children—who've let me hold them in my arms. They showed me how to grow. How to love. How to live each day with a profound sense of gratitude—that I dwell among queers, among those sensitized through difference to greater heights of compassion and effort of love and will, an effort that I believe transcends death in the end, and will ultimately provide this country with a model of real human community. Lesbian eros is my world-saving goddess. Women and children have always been my resource, my refuge, my passion and my ruin and my last best hope. I think that they are the last best hope of the earth.

To you, girlfriends, and your daughters and your sons, something I've been waiting to say for twenty years:

These stories? I wrote them for you. With you in my heart, your names and faces and bodies and spirits, known or unknown, on my hands and my tongue. I don't care if a single straight person ever reads these stories. Because I wrote them for me, and for you.

What else could any writer hope for? Just this: I hope that you like them.

*New York City, 1996*

# After the Bath

With her dress—tight fit and dark leather straps—and heels high enough for drama but not too high to dance on, she looked nice standing on the sidelines in shadows and moving bodies, her mostly finished drink, wine I guess, held perfectly between fingers. We caught eyes and nodded.

"You don't dance, do you?" She got a cigarette and looked for matches, but I plucked some out of my own pocket sooner. Years ago some woman had stumbled up in a bar somewhere, eyelids heavy with booze, and asked for a light. Oh, I said, I don't smoke. She laughed. But honey, she replied, someone like you should *always* carry matches.

It had been sweet of her, really, to say that.

I'd carried them ever since, in various parts of the world. Hopefully.

Now, I lit one. Cassie touched my hand to steady it. "Thanks."

I wanted to ask how she knew that—that I didn't dance. We recognized each other only vaguely, through parties, large dinners, friends of friends. The match did its job and I tossed it, then she was talking.

"Dell says some French girl broke your heart."

I didn't respond.

She shrugged. The dark smoke-filled place was kind to her. There were blurred old acne scars on each cheek. They must be deep because she'd used a lot of makeup. Even so she was pretty, nice lips, bright eyes. The lashes fluttered, sparking mischief.

"What's the story with Dell?"

"She thinks you're cute."

"Yucch! Damn me with faint whatchamacallit, why don't you? Anyway, she's got someone—right? Right. Of course."

"Would you like to dance?"

She thought about it. Then said yes, yes actually, that would be very nice. So we did. Two minutes into music you could bounce around to old '60s style, manic, not touching, things segued into something slow. That's when fear stabbed and I got even clumsier. But she was smooth, Cassie was, and managed somehow to balance quietly without even the appearance of precariousness, patient, seeming to enjoy herself while I fought hesitation, adjusted my stance and all, and finally pressured the small of her back to lead. It was nice, a long, long song. After some of it I realized she'd laid her head against my shoulder. Her hands had found their way under the flaps of jacket, pressed lightly on silk shirt and rib cage, and, underneath things, I was sweating.

"What do butches want?"

"Is that what I am?"

She pulled her head back a moment, eyes rolled mockingly. "Oh God, honey, come *on*." But she laughed.

"Well, what do you think?"

"I don't know—I'm curious. I mean, I like to watch you, all of you, everywhere, even when you're just standing still. I'd like to see what's going on in your head—I know it's different from what's going on in mine."

"Oh," I told her, "don't be so sure."

Well, but then again, maybe.

What do we want? I thought.

You.

But said nothing.

Just before the song ended I caressed that part of her right on top of the place where buttocks meet thighs, very lightly, barely touching at all, and could tell that she felt it. We stood around talking then. I bought her more wine, lit more of her cigarettes.

Dell came by, looking irritated in new silks and leather and linen, and a pair of fur shoes colored black and white. She said hi to Cassie, pulled me aside. "Can you lend me twenty? I met someone, I want to buy her a drink. I think she might go to bed with me tonight."

"Congratulations."

"This place is really getting on my nerves. Maybe I ought to leave. Maybe I ought to take a Xanax. You think I should? Or a Valium? But then I might fall asleep. On her, I mean. I might not be able to come. Or to make *her* come. Then the whole thing would be a disaster."

"Well, Cassie likes you."

"Oh, she's cute, but she's not my type. Besides, she lives right in my neighborhood. It might spoil things with Karen. Then Karen would get pissed and move out and I'd be a nervous wreck again, like I was after Tess left. Come to think of it, maybe I'll just go back alone. I feel like I'm getting too old to keep engaging in this search for ecstasy. It's always so futile and so incredibly disappointing."

I gave her two tens and told her it looked like a skunk had

died on her feet. She urged me to go to hell, as quickly as possible. That was okay. We were old friends and loved each other.
Dell was the epitome of a bottom: she'd fight to be the one on
her back. It was all fine and dandy with me—there was nothing
like sex between us, anyway. But I couldn't figure out what she
and Cassie would ever possibly do with each other in bed, as-
suming they made it that far, except lie side by side, full of wishes
and unfulfilled desire. When she wandered off another slow song
started—obviously the deejay was thinking about winding things
down. I didn't ask this time but gestured, in a courtly way that
made Cassie giggle, bending slightly at the waist, sweeping one
arm grandly toward the dance floor. Around us, couples clutched
in the beginnings of loss or passion, energy ebbing, fatigue set-
tling softly like extra weight in the shadows and smoke. She
cupped a hand to my ear.

"Want to fuck?"

"Yes, Cassie. But I like to say when, okay?"

As I said it, I realized it was true. And, as I realized that, I
gained all kinds of power. Moving her in slow effortless circles
and steps, dancing felt easy for the first time ever. I sensed her
melting in against me, and held both of us up, moving, while
my insides began to ache and burn.

At her place later, after the first time, she showed me all
about bubble baths. I'd rarely bothered with stuff like that before—I was strictly a shower jock, stepping out of and into towels and steady hot modulated streams; and, I told her, the gyp-
sies had a saying about baths, which they deemed an untrust-
worthy and inferior way to get clean: *Why should I soak like an
old tea bag?* But Cassie's tub was different. Deep, aged, worn but
clean, sunk like unmovable stone in the tiniest room of her tiny
apartment, something about it felt seductive. Sinking into
bubbles there was like sinking into a cloud, a pillow, a woman.
She sat primly on the polished wood toilet seat, frayed satiny

robe clutched protectively over both breasts, as if we hadn't just spent the past several hours making love—first shyly, then unrestrained raw fucking, then sweating close up against each other, and then again shy.

She was great, and made a big fuss about everything: the mixture of bubbles and lotions had to be just right, the washcloth her best, expensive skin creams were arrayed on shelves, waiting. I was touched by all this delicate consideration. It wasn't love—at least, not yet—but pleasing her had been exciting, and, now, I couldn't keep my hands off. When I stepped out dripping fragrant foams, she toweled different parts of me gently.

"I like your body."

"Yeah?"

"I like how strong you are."

I wanted to tell her that physical strength wasn't the same as a big, grown strength inside. But it occurred to me that maybe it *was*—a corresponding strength, at least, to the extent that it tangibly represented the fruits of work and a kind of courage—and, considering this silently, I reconsidered myself. That I even liked what I saw, not just tolerated it, but got some pleasure out of it as well—this image of her and me together in an age-speckled mirror—was wonderful. Something in me started to want, then, in a different, deeper way. I wondered if I'd let her make love to me some time. Not just as a tender femme service, the after-dinner drink on our sexual menu, but in a way that was scary, penetrative, requiring real trust and release. That—that was what *she* wanted, from the start: to be gotten deep inside of, to give up all control. I was glad of it. At the same time, I could barely imagine submitting or surrendering myself that way and calling it pleasure.

We *were* very different.

I dried my hands to light another cigarette and gave it over to her. She blew smoke in the direction of the mirror. In that moment she seemed very far away, exotic, her otherness electrifying.

We started to kiss and touch again. Then she was lying on her open robe, on the bed, with me full on top of her. Bubble bath soaked into sheets. She had all the right playthings, Cassie did, and plenty of latex and lube—tricks of the trade, she said, smiling in a half-hard, half-sad way. Old massage parlor girls never show up unprepared, but then again, neither did I. If I shut my eyes against her hair, touched yielding flesh, it seemed as if the bed spun round and round.

I started to fall hard then, and wanted to move all the way inside her where the world's sharp edges were muted and soft. Wanted to push in rhythm with a deep, dark, strapped-on weight that would strain her and please her, invade on invitation, a burden we both could feel, then let go of, until it brought us to some unforsaken place of home and finality and love.

What happened: We became lovers, Cassie and I. A home, lace curtains, white picket fence, apple pie in the oven on Sundays—we had all that eventually, yes, but we had it in city rooms and clubs and streets, within ourselves and each other. And, inside, there was lots more. Dyke stuff, tough and sweet. Things that cannot be described.

No one would let us adopt kids, so we took in homeless cats and dogs and, when everyone around us started dying, we cared for them in their illness, took in *their* cats and dogs after death, wept at many funerals. Another vomit-soaked sponge. Another kiss good-bye. Ceremonial washing of the hands. Bouquets of roses, incense, memorial speeches, listening over and over again to the favorite poems of dead young men. Afterwards, I'd walk her home in the dark. Protective. As if her electric femmeness was a fragile thing instead of the sure gut-deep strength it was, too good for the hard straight world around us. As if I were more than a woman myself, a fiercely muscular giant, stronger than most men.

There is a darkness inside us, and also a light. And sometimes, both are wicked; and, sometimes, both are love. What Cassie taught me, after the bath, was that pain is not the same as suffering. We can have our sorrows and use them well, not just gyrate desperately to get rid of them. We can reach in and give and take. Reach in, or out, and be taken.

Reaching in is what I did with Cassie, my woman, on many, many nights. As time went by I let her reach deep inside of me, too—oh, not often, mind you, maybe once or twice a year, like I was giving her a gift she knew to treat carefully—and she'd touch something grieving then, a darkness, a womb-tip or star. Later we'd lie glued with sweating skin. Different bodies. Different fears. And, in this age of plague, we got over each drop of our shame. We learned to use our pain. We forbade nothing and accepted all. Until straight people everywhere began to imitate us. Then they grew to full human stature, and together we saved the world.

*(1989-1990)*

# Mothers of Heroes

*Glaub* nicht, *das ich werbe.*
*Engel, und wurb ich dich auch!*
*Du kommst nicht.*

Rilke

After the army, I went up north for Tali.
There was this dream I'd had day after day, while scrubbing oil drums clean on a miserable desert military base for the Jewish State: me, swinging from a Golan apple tree's branch with a splash into something wet, the color of the Mediterranean. Then the substance coagulated into faintly human forms—her eyes, her mouth, the secret guarded crevice between her thighs I hadn't seen yet, but that surely ran into her sharp and deep.

I went because she'd written she was lonely in the autumn. I went to woo her.

Americanit, Namit told me, you're crazy. Pronounced it AH-MARE-EEE-KON-EEET, the sound harsh. Listen, stupid, don't go there, it's like a *shtetl*. Small minds in a smaller place. Come to Tel Aviv. Lots of lesbians live there, more than you think. I've got phone numbers to call. Parties to go to. It's what they say in your country—you know, New York, L.A.—liberated. Forget that bitch, she's too old anyway.

But I took buses and hitched rides, hiking from road to settlement over rock, dusty rubble and air-baked clots of brush, blinking grit from both eyes, envisioning good, cool things when the sun's hard yellow seared too close to my brain. Sour pine scent mingled with the odor of grapes, of dust. If you climbed a tree, balanced on the longest branch of one and reached with your whole arm, you'd touch Syrian air over the border. I stopped for a second and fingered her last letter, which was folded around my belt. Remembered when I had first arrived on the settlement, quiet and friendless. They grew to like me because I was strong, could do the work of a man, and offended no one. Listen, they'd ask after a while, gently teasing, persistent and curious, why don't you dance with the men sometimes? You stand apart always, strange and alone.

It was true. Until Tali sat across from me one night in the dining hall, silently eating some kind of fish with stewed tomatoes. Later that evening I went to her place. She served coffee. Watching all the half-shrewd, half-naive, unspoken things flicker across my face, she laughed. Her eyes were blue and green and gray mixed together, features frank, very Ashkenazi, with a full-lipped expressive mouth, hair bleached by the sun.

You're funny sometimes, she said. Like a sweet young man, or little boy.

There was weariness around her eyes and mouth, a tension at war with her youth—what was she, after all, twenty-seven, twenty-eight, a few years older than I? Still, the fatigue had settled already in gentle lines. It was sometimes softened, sometimes ravaged by a sadness that made her unquestionably mature, without a doubt my senior. All this seemed profoundly womanly. A thudding erupted in my chest. I wanted her before I ever loved her.

She made us coffee every night that year, talking long into the sleeting Golan evenings. The coffee was boiled mud; grounds clogged the bottom of each cup. It had a thick, hot smell, like some kind of flesh, and she served it to me with square yellow cookies filled with raisins. She asked why I had no husband, and when I told her, arched her eyebrows, then nodded silently, saying, Yes, sometimes that's the way it is. She had gone through such a phase herself, she said, in adolescence; she and another girl, her best friend, spent a night making love. But they had grown out of it quickly. All that was in the past. Later she'd been married for a while to a man she met in the service. His name was Dov. They'd had a son, but there was something wrong with the kid—he was crazy, or autistic or something—and after a while the kibbutz had him institutionalized in Haifa. Then Dov and she had split for good. Although the divorce was still pending, delayed by some high religious counsel. He lived with another woman on another kibbutz in the south, and had lost a leg up in Lebanon.

She visited her son twice a month, returning sometimes with red eyes and trembling hands. I'd touch her cheek to comfort. Oh, she'd say, it's nothing. Just a seed gone mad. I'm supposed to give babies to my people, you know, Jewish babies, to fight for Israel. I'm supposed to be the mother of as many heroes as possible. Obviously, I failed.

"Here, Tali, take!"

The apples dropped to her, dull pink and green. I perched close to a prickly trunk, shut my eyes until speckled shade burned away and I didn't see her below waiting. I felt her full mouth widening in a grin aimed only at me. There were more lines now than before, spreading from her lips' corners, across her forehead, a burgeoning network of age. But she'd been glad to see me. Stiff canvas straps dragged across my shoulders, sack heavy with fruit.

In my head I'd already descended the tree and dropped to one knee before her. The motion was so elaborate, so ceremonious, that at first it seemed mock. But, at the same time, the act made itself absolutely serious. I spread both arms in hope. What would I say? How lucky I was to be here, before they killed her, too? To have this time in which to court her? Her hands would shiver, momentarily delicate, on the apple's hard surface. And I'd say: Come away somewhere with me, let's have nothing more to do with these wars, surely everyone is sick of it by now.

"Tali, let's go to Jerusalem."

I opened my eyes and stared down.

"Okay." She said it a little mischievously, a little uncertainly. Through white light and shade her hair seemed to have turned instantly gray. Something brutal webbed her eyes. They stared back at me, curious, misted by confusion and a dark weird regret.

The city, like always, loomed suddenly ahead and up through dusty bus windows, breeze musty with age and, at the same time, freshly touched by a hint of new things, reconstitution, destruction, concrete and pine and olive groves. Arriving just before Shabbat we were caught in the frantic rush to grab transportation while the sun threatened to set—*storm before the calm,* someone in my memory had called it, *and the calm is the Queen.* But in the end, whether you wanted to make something religious of it or not, Jerusalem was just a city, really, lots of people, stones, air and dust.

We'd both been quiet on the long ride. I—wondering if and how I'd finally make love to her. She—she? Wondering whether or not she'd let me? Or thinking something else altogether? Maybe about her kid, locked up in that place in Haifa; or if the work manager would approve her request to move from the orchard to the laundry.

The apartment wasn't far from the Old City. It belonged to some friend of Tali's—from her own army days—who had gone to Be'er Sheva for the long weekend and mailed a set of keys. Soon, after a high-speed taxi ride that ended with sundown, we were upstairs there, walking over square little imitation Persian rugs, turning a lamp low, sorting through the miniature refrigerator for cucumbers, lemons, bread, making salads spiced with dabs of cheap kosher wine from a half-finished bottle. We sat cross-legged on cushions on rugs on the floor facing each other, very opposite in appearance. Here we are, she said, with you so dark from the desert, you look a hundred percent Sephardi. But your hair's short—just like a boy.

I thought of my Turkish ancestors, the one-fourth of them or so who, I imagined, had held out in their hovels and spice market stalls against all the rape and miscegenation brought by European hordes. Had held out long enough, at least, to bequeath to me the near-black curling hair, Asian cheekbones, and skin that never turned red under the sun, only brown. How different she was—so much longer in exile, in a way--the pale eyes and hair and white German skin containing barely an echo of all the dark rich violent excess that had once belonged to us, and to our people.

We ate cucumbers in lemon juice sprinkled with pepper, using torn-off hunks of bread as utensils. She swished wine in her mouth. Then looked at me with the same odd combination of curiosity, cruelty, and vulnerability I'd seen before.

"So. Are you going to love me?"

Food fell out of my mouth. Panic crushed all desire. I told her I would try.

Every woman has a different taste to her tongue, her cunt, her flesh. Tali's was musk, punctuated by a sweat of surprise and her own short breaths, feeling how fine and smooth and electric silky skin could feel against skin again, some kind of cruelty in her sated by nibbling my lips so hard she drew blood, and smeared her own mouth red. She ran a hand up my shirt, stopping at the soft protuberance of breasts, hardening nipples—I was no boy, after all. When she started to laugh and cry at the same time it made me feel tender but also somehow mean. I kept my own clothes on, shirt unbuttoned, feet bare and belt undone, while I peeled hers off. And kneeling over her on the imitation Persian rug I toyed with her a little, pretending to examine all the inches of her nakedness, where the hips were wider and fleshy, inner thighs trembling, arms thick, breasts marked by the pulling of an infant's mouth, eyes shut now in a kind of shame, and the big delicate womanly hands that teased me too, and, while I fought for control, threatened to undo me. I held her head still by her thick, fair hair, pulled it back to suck hard on her neck until a red welt rose, licked her ear until she moaned for real, and when I was sure that all the laughing had stopped and tears dried, when her cunt slid along my pants leg leaving wet thick marks, I fucked her with my hands and mouth fearlessly, shamelessly, sensing that, for just those minutes, I was no longer so hopelessly peripheral to things, that in this brief urgency of moments was a way for us both to be inside something more than just each other, to fuck our way into belonging, into the insular sealed-off astonishing singular loneliness of ourselves and of our people. No, she said. Then, yes, and, My love, my love! Finished! Finished! Finished! Yelling out loud. When she'd stopped moving so hard, her breaths came easier, sweat sprinkled her forehead. She sobbed very gently. Then she pushed me away and out of her roughly, like I was some unwanted servant, rolled over and began to crawl, then stood and stumbled to the bathroom.

I lay there on the unfamiliar rug unbuttoned, unbuckled, and I heard water running. Something in me was crying, too, sending sporadic silent drops along my face, but I didn't know what or why.

She bathed a long time. I listened to the sobbing, scrubbing, splashing. After a while, just the matter-of-fact gush of draining water.

She appeared neatly towel-wrapped but still more or less

dazed, leaning against a door jamb. It was as if she'd been exposed to some disease that only immediate hygiene could intercept, so she'd scrubbed like a demon until the suspect top layer of skin was nearly gone, steamed herself sweating and raw.

"Now," she said, "I'm afraid."

"Of what, Tali?"

She shrugged. Then her lips pursed in the burnished perspiring face, and her smell wafted my way, clean hair, soap.

"What about you? You want me to do that to you?"

"No, Tali."

"Why not?"

"Maybe I'm afraid, too."

It wasn't true, and we both knew it. What I wanted, really, was to maintain whatever thin barrier there still was between us because the barrier gave me power, a fragile power that might have been crushed by a breath, or the touch of her tongue. She turned to put some clothes on. Later, silently, we shared a last sip of wine, she smoked a foul kibbutz-issue cigarette that burned as if composed of dried wood chips, and she fell asleep under a blanket on the sofa while I lay on the rug, surrounded by half-eaten plates of cucumber salad and drying crusts of bread. It was cold outside, the way Jerusalem nights are, and I curled up fetally before dreaming.

I had more a nightmare than a dream, something to do with my old home in America: I'd had a frustrating, lengthy trip back through deserts and waters and crumbling mansions, but when I arrived there was a war, everyone fleeing something terrible, and I wanted desperately to retrace all my steps. For some reason this was impossible, so I stood there, frozen, while all the panicked people passed me by. And, repeatedly, I tried to scream, or make a sound, but couldn't. I woke in real physical pain because Tali was biting my thighs. She had somehow worked my belt off and the pants down around both knees and was biting the flesh hard, here and there, making bruises. I grabbed her head but she didn't budge. Then for some reason I gave up and just lay back, silently wanting to cry, locked both hands behind my own head to cushion it until the knuckles ached, and I let her hurt me. I hated it but felt somehow that I deserved it; after all, I'd helped her commit abomination. But she stopped biting and starting licking, sucking, kissing, really emphatically, saying that it had been too long and now, finally, here was someone she could love. After a while, I didn't want to protest.

When we returned from Jerusalem Tali got her transfer to the laundry, I continued with my old job in the apple orchards, and we didn't see each other much. At first I'd knock on her door every evening, like old times. But she wasn't there, or didn't answer. She let me in only once. The coffee was thin, and lukewarm, and she didn't offer any fruit or cookies. We were quiet for a while—I, curious and wounded; she fiddling with her kerosene heater, ignoring me. Finally I got up some courage.

"Tali, what's with you? Can we talk about things?"

She turned slowly, then slapped my face hard. It was just the excuse I needed to leave, racing across dark stony ground to my own little shack where, chest aching with tears that wouldn't spill, I cowered under coarse blankets in a metal-frame bed.

After that we never spoke. Once in a while, if I met her in the dining hall food line, or passed her on the way to pick up some laundry, our eyes would meet, briefly, and she'd nod. Several times we found each other at the roadside bus stop, heading in different directions. I'd heard through the active, heartless, insatiably nosy settlement grapevine that things were no longer quite so hopeless with her son, he'd taken a turn for the better, and her presence was required more often at the institution in Haifa. Increasingly, when I had free time, I'd leave for Namit's place in Tel Aviv. I didn't much like Namit—and the truth is that neither one of us found any love in that city, although we found plenty of women who were curious—but she was the one ally I had.

Winter was freezing in the Golan, hot humidity further south. I had a flu for months, felt weak and delirious off and on, couldn't work much. One Friday I took a bus to Haifa. I went to the institution where I knew they kept Tali's kid and stood outside the lead-and-concrete door gazing at the surveillance hole, feeling distinctly small and harmless, until they buzzed me in.

I gave a phony name, told them I was Tali's cousin, and the nurse, who had that dull, passive pouting look of an unpredictably sadistic civil servant, led me down yellowish-gray corridors that smelled of human shit. Once in a while, from behind closed metal doors pierced at eye level by wire-protected observation windows, you could hear children cry.

The room she led me to was at the end of a hallway plastered here and there by posters of flowers and sunrises colored in a kind of wildly bright, overprocessed Kodak dementia. The heavy door was opened. Inside, in a little space reeking with sour milk and urine, Tali sat on the bare floor next to a man with one leg, while a fiercely handsome boy in soaked diapers pounded his bandage-padded head against a wall.

It was the kid who saw me first, pausing for a second to turn to the door with a kind of animal instinct, a brief flash of warning, maybe, in his blue eyes. Then he screamed once, twice, monotonously, and went back to pounding his head. His mother and father stared.

Tali confronted me in the hall, around a corner. Her face was a weary lack of expression crisscrossed by premature lines. Her voice was flat and throaty.

"They said we can take him home soon. Dov and I are getting back together."

"Why, Tali?" I heard myself sound like a faraway echo, humble, stupid. "I'm the one you said you could love."

"Oh," she said, "that doesn't matter."

Something smashed my cheek and I grabbed wildly for support, found none, slid down along a bright bubbling poster smelling rotten food and diaper shit. When my eyes could focus again I stared up at Dov, who was swaying over me on one leg, elbow to wall, holding in his other hand a hard plastic flesh-toned prosthetic limb. It had a knee joint and an ankle joint and five little bumps on the end, like toes. The biggest toe was smeared with red. I touched my face, felt dripping blood. But he had lost a big piece of himself for this country and for our people, and probably for Tali, too. In that moment I sensed that he and I were more similar than different. He had just smashed my face, but I didn't even blame him. We both would go to war when necessary. Both of us loved a woman.

I left the settlement and stayed at Namit's place for a while, did odd jobs through the spring, until the weather turned viciously hot and Tel Aviv became one big cloud of auto fumes and exhaustion and, for the first time in months, I started to think seriously about America. It had once been my home and still might be again; and, while I was sure to be in a sort of irrevocable exile there, there was also the possibility that I could work hard, and find someone to love.

I walked along the city beaches at night that summer trying to decide, kicking through damp sand, sometimes crying. It did not make sense to exile myself from a place and a people that I would have died for. On the other hand, it would be easier for me to die for my people than to have a life among them. The truth was that I wanted what they did: peace, security, a fertile existence. But I wanted other things, as well. I wanted them to love me, too—not as someone beaten into a standard straight configuration, but as myself, as all that I was—and that, I finally understood, would never happen.

Namit scoffed at my confusion. Listen, she sneered, impatient but with a surprising down-to-earth wisdom, just do what makes you happy. Stay. Or go. It doesn't really matter. You think it does, but it doesn't. You're still a queer. You're still here, in the world.

At the airport, waiting, I visited the bathroom. I took out a marker and, on the wall, drew a heart with an arrow through it pointing to Tali's name and to mine. Then I scribbled lines over it. Thinking of her, I barely felt disturbed. I wondered if I'd ever even loved her.

America was there and of course I did go back, finding it changed after the years, but still fresh and strange somehow. I worked hard, lost my tan and my old beliefs, then after a long time fell in love again. My lover and I blended easily into the free, cluttered fabric of a big, big city.

I still thought every day of the tiny country I had left so sadly. The sorrow was only mine, I knew. Probably, in truth, my people had never wanted to claim me; they were glad to see me go. Yet they were irrevocably mine, and I theirs—despite ourselves, despite the mess of everything, as surely as the loss and sadness, as surely as I had made love to Tali on a rug in an apartment in Jerusalem—and, when bad news of the Middle East spilled off newspaper headlines, I felt their terrible aloneness and my own solitude acutely, woke up some nights shot through with a kind of frustrated terror: that the land would be attacked again and I would not be there with boots and a gun, in a gas mask, in a sealed room, alongside them.

I thought of Tali sometimes, and wondered how things had gone for her, and Dov, and the kid. There were nights I dozed off with a half-dream of her reaching toward me across some wretched expanse. Sometimes, before sleeping, I'd reach out too. And then, like angels, we'd touch.

*(1977)*

# A Room, in a Stone House, in Spain

When she winked I followed her into a laundry near the Pâtisserie de Tunis. Crazy clothes spilled from her *panier* to the machine basin: dyed purples, beige faded to grayish yellow stained with mustard and red wine. She held up a tiny green shirt.

"My son."

It was half proud, half apologetic. I asked how old but kept smiling, and she seemed to relax then, told me four years last month.

"Nice birthday party?"

She grinned; I spoke French terribly. It seemed a wise expression, not cutting at all, white teeth glowing suddenly against the background of smooth light-brown skin, full lips tinted red. Our hair was the same color, almost black. Mine was short though, hers past her shoulders, and I wondered for a minute, disturbed, whether it was the similarity or the difference that had led me thoughtlessly this close.

"Pardon. It's your first time here?"

I nodded.

"France pleases you?"

"No."

"You're Spanish? Italian?"

"I'm a Jew."

Ah, she said, as if that explained something quite puzzling. Then, with a mixture of discomfort and relief, "You know, so am I."

She shook some faintly blue detergent into the stew of clothes. Soon the first cycle rattled away, cloth spun wetly, momentarily meshed together, made vibrating rainbow streaks against the round machine window. She had sad dark eyes that I wanted to kiss shut. I wanted to kiss her neck.

"Matches?"

I didn't smoke but found some anyway in a pocket, lit her Gauloises nonfilter, and waited almost breathlessly until she puffed out the first heavy cloud and cocked her head at me, shrewdly evaluating. She nodded once, accepting my homage as her rightful due. I leaned against another machine. Felt something changeless in me spin through the dissipating smoke over washers and dryers, rise feather-light to peer coolly, painlessly down on the wintery damp streets of this shabby *arrondissement,* and on her and me.

Somewhere a dryer creaked open. Steam poured out, with a smell of sodden cloth. Then doubt cleared from her face and she smiled back at me, softly teasing, puffing doughnut-shaped clouds until I blushed and looked away. In the too-large woolen sweater and sagging denims, American style, she seemed terribly small for a moment, and frail, never mind the tough filterless hanging from her lips. I noticed that her boots were worn at the toe, but a good black leather; that the scarf she'd arranged around her neck was bright multicolored silk. There was pride in that, there was vanity. Somehow, too, there was danger. I got a burst of courage then. The changeless thing inside that made me different, strange—like some creature out of place and time—

nodded, and moved me a little closer.

Her apartment was small, very shadowy and old, in a creaking building just a few streets away and a few flights up, so it made perfect sense to help her carry her laundry there. Inside, it smelled of ginger and other things. She turned lamps on, drew curtains, shutting out the night. Then it made sense for me to light her another Gauloises, and for her to serve me tea.

I watched the bright scarf disappear into some small vestige of kitchen where she ran faucets, clattered with pots and silverware, and I settled back in a worn old sofa and looked and sniffed around. Not just ginger I smelled, but the yellow paste of turmeric, ripe raisins, crushed almonds, salty oiled olive skin mixed with the scent of sweating flesh and powder, of damp city streets. I thought immediately of flat bread and grape leaves. Then imagined going into the kitchen and walking up behind her, reaching gently around to hold her breasts. The room and the smells made me terribly homesick—although for what place, in what time, I didn't even know—but tears abruptly filled my eyes.

She came back holding a big tray full of cups and saucers, and I had to brush them away—the tears, I mean—just as quickly; they couldn't have been explained. At least not in words. And, for the moment, a purely physical fear pounded me back and forth: she probably wanted someone more refined on the outside, a lot tougher on the inside, more worldly, someone free and careless and pretty. I was tired, inattentive and numb from all the traveling, the wandering. My touch might disappoint her.

"Sugar?"

"Thanks."

On one shelf was a tarnished old menorah, base crusted with white wax. Bound bunches of dried wild flowers. Over the traces of an ancient arch, now filled in by wall and poorly plastered, Jesus hung from his cross—rough-cut wooden feminine form twisted in a distinctly Spanish agony: ribs protruding, slender muscles and internal organs striated clearly against the dark-brown skin, face framed by black hair, blood streaming over the closed, anguished eyes. So clearly out of place and time here, in cuisine-conscious, style-conscious France. I stared at it a long time, then back at her, full of questions and surprise.

She sipped her tea, amused. I suddenly understood.

"Your people—Marranos?"

She nodded at me, at Jesus. "Yes, sure, long ago. They brought him with them from Spain."

"Your parents were born here?"

"No. Morocco, Algeria, everywhere."

That was all she knew, she told me. Anyway, the past was the past. It hardly mattered. Her family did not speak of it much.

Ah, I said, as if I knew the story. I didn't, really; I barely knew my own. From Spain some had managed to make it to Turkey, Moldavia, Romania, had met and mixed with Russians and Germans and Poles. How much by consent, how much by duress, no one alive would know. And few were still alive.

"Would you like to see my son?"

"No."

"Why not?"

My French was too poor to explain. I barely knew why not myself—and how to say, anyway, that I wanted to know her only as a woman, not a mother. That I wanted just certain pieces of her, now, nothing more, for reasons and terrors of my own. She seemed momentarily disappointed, then just shrugged and sat.

She began folding clothes, plucking baby socks from the overflowing *panier* and rolling them into tiny white pairs. It occurred to me that she was right: the past might not matter at all—at least to us here, in this room, this life, in the flesh. And wasn't it, after all, her flesh that mattered to me right now, and her eyes and breasts and lips? That mattered much, much more than any concept of motherhood, or peoplehood, any gaping erasure of history?

I put my tea down unfinished, and stood and went around behind the sofa, ran unsure hands through her hair, bent to press a cheek against it, began massaging her shoulders.

That's sweet, she said, just like that. That's very, very sweet.

Later we were both standing somewhere else on a worn old rug, halfway between the menorah and Jesus, facing each other, very close. She seemed much easier with it all, much more relaxed than I, telling me just when to kiss her, how much and how deep, and how good it felt, sometimes sighing to close her eyes. When they opened I'd examine them—looking for something, I thought, some sign of love or fear or memory—and I noticed they were green-brown with flecks of orange and gray in them, like mine.

"Would you like to come to bed with me?"

Her hands fluttered very softly along my hips, persuading. What about your son? I asked, and she said, simply, It's late, he's asleep. Then her hands became bold and pulled me right against her, rocking us both back and forth, so that after a while she began to breathe very quickly, I no longer felt tentative, or worried about being too gentle or too rough, and the whole standing, rocking motion we made together developed an urgency and recklessness. I could feel the control of things shifting to me, and the momentary sweet anonymous helplessness of her need, as if there was something that could burst right out of me, through my skin, my clothes, through hers, and reach deep to touch some hungry, wanting thing inside her.

Down a hall with old tiled floor, in a closet-sized bedroom, in the mess of sheets and a warm tired colorless quilt that smelled like her, between lamplight and cheap shades and curtains that kept out the cool, damp breeze of night, she took off her own clothes. I began to strip too, then stopped, the dark cold strange little thing inside, the thing that could deform me sometimes and save me at other times, begging me, now, to go only so far. Seeing this, she smiled. It was a gentle smile, utterly soft and knowing and female. She opened a drawer and took things out. In the dull light I watched, surprised and almost amused, smelled leather, aluminum buckles, rubber forms—silicone, latex—of different sizes and colors. She brushed past me naked and I smelled her hair and flesh. She lit her own cigarette.

Okay, she said, you choose.

Then she sat on the bed and watched, smoking. A tiny smile remained.

I was afraid but intrigued. And admired her for doing this. Here, by asking me to choose what I'd fuck her with, she'd force me to reveal at least a little. How did I want to represent myself, to her, tonight? Big and hard and dangerous, too much to take? Or small, playful, energetic, inventive? Or something in-between? Knowing that, this first time, I'd choose only what I could handle. In the end I chose and undressed partially, strapping the harness around my naked waist. It had been years since I'd used one of these. Something hot and stinging blurred my eyes. But I remembered without fumbling. The trick was in the tightness. Everything else just a motion that fits.

We pressed together in a half-dark, half-lit, fleshy, textured place you had to close your eyes to see and feel: dark red behind tight-shut eyelids, brown nipples, the musky sea smell when I kissed the insides of her thighs, understanding all over again why in Spanish and Ladino the word for conch shell is the same as the word for cunt.

I made love to her, pressing inside when she was ready with the toy that wasn't really a toy. Just a tool I'd chosen that might hurt her sometimes, or sometimes give her pleasure. But I was more enchanted than I knew. Causing pain was the farthest thing from my mind—though I did want to hear her cries and, when I did, felt myself melting and almost lost control.

Cars sloshed through puddles on the city streets. Far-off sirens wailed from a Premier Secour ambulance, passing by into silence. She was covered with sweat and a soft, soft relief, opening my shirt, kissing in a straight line down along my body. No, I told her, no, there's more isn't there? And I pulled her back underneath between damp flesh and sheets and pushed simply, easily, inside her again. All in the motion and, this time, I had the rhythm and the feeling back again. I half-crouched over her and could smell olive oil somewhere, held her feet on my shoulders, whispered ungrammatically in several languages that here we were, two women, in a little room somewhere in a little country, and we were both safe, what a miracle. On the bed I could feel her shudder, tense, swell. This time she moaned long and deep, a sound beyond relief or mere pleasure, like aching, or crying.

Later I let her fuss with all the buckles and straps herself. She shoved them unceremoniously off the side of the bed. The little hard cold strange thing inside gave off warning signals the closer she got to belly and cunt. I held her head in both hands, guiding, forbidding, encouraging, as if I really could control her and myself. I spread her hair out right, left, to cover each thigh, until the hair was a cape safely swaddling me, and I stroked her head and watched until my eyes flicked shut and I couldn't watch anymore.

She slept off and on, and until 2:30 A.M. I held her. Then I got restless and she must have sensed it, sitting against pillows soaked with the smell of us both, searching along the nightside table for a cigarette. I reached across her for matches. Struck one alive in the dark, perfectly, dutifully. In the sudden light, like a firefly tail, thought I saw tortured brown Jesus on the wall, watching. The Gauloises tip glowed orange ash. In stilted French we talked some—she about her job, and old girlfriends and boyfriends, and I told her a little about America, Israel, the army—but what we said, really, I wouldn't quite remember. In the dark her eyes looked large, glittering with a kind of humor. Every once in a while, between thick musky puffs of smoke, she'd run a finger along my lips and pout, and giggle. When she finished the cigarette we started to kiss again. I glanced sideways to the cluttered nightside table—an alarm clock, an ashtray, a last fading ember—imagined it a prowling, glowing eye riding weightless over the bed, urging us on. She slid underneath very easily and naturally, as if we'd been doing this every night for years, and pulled my head down until her mouth was right up against my ear. "Will you—try to put your hand inside me?" Oh, I said, can I, may I please?

Afterwards I slept and had a dream—of me and her long ago, on a pallet, on a floor, in some hot and foreign climate. The air smelled of firewood and smoke, dried fruit, livestock, hot baked stone. A single blast of conch shell reverberated through the dust of a sun-seared afternoon, called the faithful to prayer. She was then as she was now, but I was different— physically, maybe, or in some other way; and whether male or female I could not tell. There was the sense of life being difficult but often satisfying. Bitter. Frightening. Treacherous and mystifying. Yet expansive somehow, full of sun and air, curiosity, occasional laughter, love. We had a child, a dark little toothless laughing boy. On the bed, in the afternoon heat trapped by stone floor and walls, echoing with the last almost-musical blast of conch shell, air filled with a smell of almonds and of raisins, animal hides, a child's dusty pounding bare feet. Cattle moaned. Outside, people rolled in pits of crushed dark grape, making love, intoxicated, clothes drenched as if with blood.

I woke and wanted to tell her but she was sleeping. The tiniest hint of sunrise had seeped through curtains. I slid out of bed feeling tired and anxious, as if I'd lost something important, and would never get it back.

Still, I had to pause and admire the way she breathed so fluidly, delicately, thin shoulders sighing in untouched perfect rhythm. I noticed, in gray light mixing with the closed dark fleshiness of the room, that there were faint stretch marks along the sides of her breasts, across her slender belly. She was a mother, irrevocably. It seemed to me utterly regrettable, yet somehow magnificent.

I was still glad, though, that I'd refused to see her child. This—a pretty woman, naked in bed and peacefully asleep after love-making, skin faintly marked by life and other women and by a few men and even children, this was the way I wanted to remember her some day. I certainly didn't mean to get into it any deeper. Kids were a hook. You could ignore them and thus stop things between you and another woman dead in their tracks; or you could set an endless roller coaster of emotion going by opening your arms to them. But, in either case, once the designation Mother got tossed into the pot, the relationship stew would never be the same. On the one hand, I had been traveling too long and was exhausted; it would be nice to know her name and, if she agreed, to spend a few harmless days with her here in Paris. But on the other hand there was the problem of the kid; and, after all, I told myself, I had had enough of mothers. Now, thankfully, love was not involved. I could simply avoid that kind of trouble, could quietly move on.

We always like to believe we are in control.

I stepped into the hallway, upper arm rubbing along the wall for direction. In the boxlike bathroom with a big colonial tub taking up most of the space I found and pulled a dangling string until a single dull lightbulb switched on, sparkling against a water-speckled mirror that I avoided. My own reflection was the last thing I wanted to see. I did check her little cabinet, though, for drugs. Sleeping pills, tranquilizers—these things were as easy to get in Paris as Croque Monsieurs. After months and years of the peculiarly volatile hyper-consciousness required for survival in the Middle East, this kind of readily obtainable oblivion was like candy to me and, since arriving in France, I'd turned to it often. Not even for sleep, but for a pleasurable, hazy tranquility that blurred the edges of each moment. Predictably, she had several bottles of prescription things in low dosages, and I took one of each. Then perched on the bathtub ledge, let my shirt fall off, and ran hot water. The building's pipes started grinding bitterly behind old walls. I glanced up at the lightbulb, lost track of time, slowly cranked on the cold water, too, and, after an eternity, slid down, almost drowning into the steamy enveloping bath. I rested my head against a faucet. Remembered the dream. Something about it was disturbing, had made me want to cry. It came back: the smell of raisins and of almonds, of hot baked stone, and a woman and a child and a southern climate that was mine, all mine.

*Let me stay here with you,* I breathed into the steam. *Let me stay here with you like I did in that past life, in your house that smells of ginger and turmeric and raisins and almonds, grape leaves, flat bread, a child, our people. Don't make me leave. Don't send me away again. This is my skin, my climate. Hold my head between your breasts. Let me find that place once more.*

The urge to cry dissipated, drifted. A serene drowsiness crept, seeping, from my toes up, spun me in a web of tranquil sleepless relief.

Was it real or hallucination, the brown sleepy-eyed boy standing between toilet and doorway, yawning, asking in a barely comprehensible baby French, Was I one of Mommy's friends? I heard myself tell him, Sure I am. Fumbled for the plug. Listened to the water start draining away in sorry sucking noises. He rubbed his lumpy brown bellybutton. Stuck a thumb between his lips, watching me calmly.

"Mommy's asleep?"

"Yes."

"Why?"

"She's tired," I told him, "sometimes big people get tired." All the water drained and suddenly I didn't feel serene any more, just small and beaten, shivering naked without the shield of steam and heat around me. He was a pretty little boy, her coloring, her eyes. There was something familiar about him. Then I knew: I had seen him before, both recently and long ago. He was the child of my dream. Of course. Utterly familiar, though I had tried not to know him. Probably unavoidable—in fact, inescapable—no matter how much I tried to evade him, or her, or whatever fully fleshed present-day life we might enjoy, together, between the shards of past and future.

I'd taken too many pills and my eyelids were starting to roll down, down. Before they shut completely I heard her voice in the background—sternly questioning, in French I could not quite understand, a mother's tone—and I ran cold water, splashed myself awake, rose unsteadily until I was more than twice his size, standing there, naked and dripping, a fumbling foreign woman. Exhaustion filled me. Panic withered away inside. Then I was rooted to the colonial bathtub, the French ceramic spot, smiling. Trapped by myself, and by a woman and a child. Her voice came closer. I could leave soon, yes. But it would be nice to know her name.

I reached for a half-clean towel. The boy blinked and yawned. When I wrapped it all around I noticed that his little dick was pointing straight out at me while he yawned, like an invitation, or a warning.

*(1979)*

# Her Marathon

*I wrote this story for Julie DeLaurier.*

*All events herein are fictional, except for the New York City Marathon and the Women's Mini-Marathon (once sponsored by L'eggs, now sponsored by Advil, under the auspices of the New York Road Runners Club). I have used these events here solely in a fictional context.*

*All characters herein are fictional, too, with the exception of the great American marathon runner Alberto Salazar. I use him here in an imaginary way, as a dream figment or a sort of divinity—and with all due respect. I have never met Mr. Salazar, and do not know if he is a child of Chango.*

I was drunk sick, I was bleeding. Not the kind that comes from somebody smashing your face in, but the bleeding inside when you're hurt, when you're down, and this whole damn city's like a bunch of sharks smelling something wounded, circling you to bite, swimming around. Stare in the mirror and you say to yourself, Baby, you look like shit. Which I did. Hell, it was true. Like some piece of worm shit crawled out from under a log, squirming around all white, all stripped of the natural color God gave her, crawling in the sunlight. I brushed my teeth. I put lipstick on. Said to myself, Girlfriend, you still got about an ounce of pride left, so get your ass downstairs and over to the Walgreen's and get some of that stomach-settle shit before you puke all over.

The kid was sleeping. So was Needa and her fucking friends from the grocery shift, snoring, burping beer dreams in a chair, on the sofa, every which place. I tiptoed over bodies. Wrapped keys in a hanky. Then I went down the three flights into autumn, cold sunlight, Sunday.

Usually up here on Sundays you could roll an old empty down First Avenue and it wouldn't touch nothing. Only this day was different. Stepping out of the building was like being caught up in a big screaming people circus of arms and shouts. They stayed on the sidewalk, jammed in like fish so you couldn't shove through them to cross the street, you could not hardly move, and some guy's got a radio, and around me every once in a while they're saying, really hushed, *He's coming.*

"He's coming."

"He's coming."

There were sirens, red and yellow-white flashes, shadows of light on the empty paved street vivisected by a yellow line, by a pale blue line, and this buzz got loud everywhere around and through me and then, like a bandaid, stopped the bleeding.

"Who?" I whispered. "Who's coming?"

"The first man."

"Who?"

"The first runner."

Still, a big sick was in my belly, threatening to lurch out, and there was a part of me thinking, I gotta cross the street, get to Walgreen's. So I started to push, try to make it through the crowd. Some dyke turned to me looking nasty and says, "*Mira,* bitch, stay where you are. Did your mother raise you in a cave? I mean, have some respect! This is the marathon."

Any other day I would have clawed out her fucking eyeballs. But the sirens, the tires, got closer. Bringing with them the whirling, spattering lights, bright motorcade chrome, October wind, silent feet. And a scream rose up from the whole shark city, from its garbage tins and sidewalk cement, from the sweat and love and hope of human bodies, from my own insides.

Then I saw him.

No, I didn't see him, I caught him with my eyes. But he escaped.

He was tall and dark, with dark eyebrows and burning black eyes and a fierce young face, and he ran like some great hot flame on the breath of the wind. When he breathed he breathed in the air of the world so that there was nothing left for us. His feet were fast, a blur, a howl. He ran like God. Chango, I said silently, here he is, your son. In that second all the air of the world was gone. I choked. I thought I would die. Tears came to my eyes.

"Salazar!" someone yelled.

"It's Salazar!"

"Salazar!"

"Bravo!"

"*Viva!*"

"*Viva,* Salazar!"

He passed, spattering pavement with his sweat.

The sun blew cold, sirens and screams twisted around, gathered me up into them. Until I fell down into the center of the storm. It blinked up at me—one-eyed, black and fierce. *Woman,* it said, *you must burn thus. Light a candle. Save your life.*

"Help me!" I sobbed. And bit through my lip.

When I opened my eyes the sun had stopped moving. People yelled, cheered, pressed in against me. Radios blared. My tears were dry so I yelled and cheered too, and wind whipped leaves down the street as more runners came by, more and more, thousands, until it seemed that they filled the whole city, and that all of us, all of us, were running.

I stayed there screaming for hours. Until the sun started to fade a little and I lost my voice. Then I stayed there still, way past the time when this guy with the radio said, Okay *oye* everybody, he won, Salazar won, didn't nobody come close, plus he set a world record.

But here, on our side of town, was still most of the rest of the runners. Fifteen, twenty thousand. And they all had plenty more to go, more than ten miles the radio guy said, before they got to the finish.

There were people skinnier than toothpicks running, and a guy wearing pink rabbit ears. Men and girls, both wearing those mesh shirts so light you can see right through, and men and girls both wearing T-shirts with their names magic-markered on front and back: HELENA, says one; BERNIE'S BOY, says another. And as they went past everyone yells out, "Go, Helena!" and "Attaway, Bernie's Boy!" There were old people running, too, and daughters, and mothers, black and white and every shade in between, from every one of these United States and from plenty of other countries—France and Mexico and Belgium and Trinidad, you had better believe it—so many people, and not all of them real fast, nor all of them skinny. Some even looked like me.

I waited, screaming with no sound until the crowd began to disappear, lights went on in windows all around, and the sun was going down. There weren't so many runners now, but still lots of people walking. Some limping. In the shadows you could see how some had these half-dead, half-crazy expressions. "All right, honey," I croaked out about every two minutes to another one, "all right, honey, keep going, you're gonna finish." Pretty soon I realized I was shivering and went upstairs.

The kid was watching TV, eating Fritos. All of Needa's friends were gone, and Needa was pissed. Where you been? she said. You look like something the tide washed in, and how come you didn't get no more beer?

I told her shut up, have some respect, today is the marathon. The what? she says. The marathon, I said, the marathon, and if you didn't spend your weekends being mean and bossing me around like some man, you coulda seen Salazar run. What the fuck, she grumbled. But then she shrugged. We didn't fight after all—even though, truth be told, I was feeling pretty sick of her just then and I wouldn't have minded. I mean, we never even did it anymore.

I picked the kid up and danced him around the room a little until he laughed. I thought about how handsome he was, bright smile and big black eyes the girls would all fight and die over some day, and how he was doing okay with the alphabet in kindergarten, too, and the teachers said real nice things about him, and other kids wanted to be his friend. Then I thought, squeezing him close, what a fucking miracle it was that such a great kid had come out of a loser like me. Fact of the matter being that neither me nor his father is all that great in the looks department. Neither one of us remembered, really, why we ever tried that boy-girl shit in the first place—I always did like the ladies better. Maybe just got curious. Then, first thing I know I'm about to pop, mister father there blows, and, later, there's Needa and me. She came on so sweet to me at first, so butch and pretty. Now life was more or less her working and me working, paying rent, keeping things clean, getting the kid back and forth to school, on weekends some videos, arguments, TV, beer. And neither one of us with a nice word or touch for the other. Nights, I'd get filled with a sudden big darkness when all the lights went out. Filled with a power so black and brown and green. Oggun, Yemaya. Iron, water, a big washing-over foaming waving ocean sadness. Then plain exhaustion that pressed my eyelids down. Needa would already be snoring. I'd turn my back, start to dream. In the morning, would not remember.

"Stop dancing your son around the room," snapped Needa, "you'll turn him into a fucking fairy. Come here, kid. We're gonna get a couple movies."

"Fine," I told her, "look who's talking. Biggest bull I ever knew. Go on, both of you. Get a couple of Real Man movies. Get a couple of Let's Kill Everyone In Sight things, why don't you. Fill his head with a bunch of real *machitos* getting their guts blown out."

When they left I cleaned up Fritos and beer cans. Got some frozen chicken out. Then, halfway through soaking it in a pot of warm water, wiped my hands with a fresh white cloth, lit a couple candles, offered up a plate of half-thawed gizzards. I stay away from the powers, mostly, but that night felt different. Kneeling in front of the plate for at least a little proper respect, red candles, white candles dripping, watching thin pieces of ice melt off the gizzards and the thawing organs swim in remains of their own dark blood, I thought again about Salazar. I wondered if he ran so hard and so fast that when he won his feet were crusted with blood. I remembered things my grandma told me, long ago, when I'd walk out laughing into the sun of a hot, sweet summer morning. About the happiness of the air filled with voices and smells, joy of loving, the ferocity of vengeance and of hate, how to heal what you care for, how to ruin an enemy. The holiness of sacrifice.

Not that I even did it right.

When they want live roosters, they don't mean half-thawed chicken gizzards. But it was all for the fire, hungry, holy fire that doesn't die, even when the world tries to kill it, that stays alive, eating, eating—I offered it truly in my heart, and God sees everything.

The next morning Needa groaned and jammed her head under a pillow when the alarm clock rang early. I tiptoed around, stuck on a pair of sweatpants, socks, old tennis sneakers, one of her used-up sweatshirts. It was cold out, wind coming off the river. Sun wasn't even up yet. I held keys in the space between fingers and balled up my hand like a fist, like a metal-bristling weapon, and when I started to run I could feel the fat bobbling around my stomach and arms and hips and thighs, heavy and disgusting, bringing me a little bit closer to the ground each time the skin folds flopped up and down. After a couple minutes I thought I was gonna die. I had to stop and gasp and walk. Then when I could breathe okay I'd run as fast as I could another half a minute or so, stop and gasp and walk a while, then run again. I did this about fifteen, twenty minutes. Until snot dripped to my lip, and my face was running wet in the cold, blotching Needa's sweatshirt. I started to cry. Then I told myself, Shut up you. It worked; the tears stopped. I went back inside, climbed stairs with legs that were already numb and hurting, and made everybody breakfast. Needa growled her way through a shower and padded around with a coffee cup making wet footprints everywhere, watching *Good Morning America.*

"There he is," she grumbled, "there's your man, your Salazar."
I ignored that sarcasm.

But I was struck there in the kitchen, making sure the kid's toast didn't burn. I told Needa to tell me what they were saying.

"They're saying about how he won yesterday. You know, the race. Guy set a fucking world record or something."

I wanted to run and see but couldn't.

That's how the weeks went: me getting up early in the dark, going to bash my fat brains out trying to run, getting breakfast for everyone, showering when they were all finished with the bathroom, getting Needa to work and the kid to school and then getting myself to work. My eyes started hurting bad from being open extra long. My legs were sore, thighs feeling like they were all bruised and bloodied on the inside, calves with pinpricks of pain searing through them. Needa noticed me limping around all the time, and laughed. What's with you, girl? You think you gonna be in the Olympics or something? You think you gonna run that marathon?

Finally, one Saturday, I went to see Madrita.

She took out the cards and beads and shells, there in her

little place in the basement, pulled all the curtains closed so everything was cozy and safe like your mother's womb. Outside, it rained. She was trained the old way, did everything absolutely right, took her time. After a while I asked her, Well, how does it look?

"Sweetheart, you gotta lotta obstacles."

Hey, I told her, that ain't exactly news.

She sighed. "You gotta stop worrying about the home. Home's gonna take care of themselves, you be surprised. Lots of rage and pain but lots of love too. See, sweetheart, you can do what you want only it's difficult. First, purify yourself."

"Purify? Myself?"

"What I said."

She wrote down all the stuff I had to get—white and red roses and violet water and rose water, mint, coconut, a bunch of sunflowers and herbs and things, and made me memorize how to do the bath right. Then she told me go up to the little shop the Jew man has, here's the address, he's one of them from Spain and he knows the right things, even *babalaus* goes there for supplies. And while you're there get a couple of pieces of camphor, sweetheart, and some fresh mint leaves. Put them in a little bag, pin it inside your bra, it'll keep you healthier. You got a cold coming on.

Needa wasn't too happy about the bath water sitting all night, reeking herbs and flower petals, before *I* got into it— first!—the next morning. Yaaah, she grumped, you and that devil shit. Ever since the marathon. Makes me feel like I'm living with some fucking boogy. But listen, woman: Don't you go casting no spells on me.

I was stripping sweaty sweats and socks to bathe. Caught her staring out the corner of my eye, and bared my teeth. Then she rubbed my naked butt, friendly-like, and the both of us laughed.

The mornings got darker, closer to winter, but every once

in a while I'd wake up easier when the alarm hit, sometimes even with a feel of burning red excitement in my chest and throat, like the running was something pleasurable, good, a gift. Truth is that it did feel good some mornings. I'd breathe splendidly. Thighs move like water, arms pump rhythm. The feet did not want to stop. Those days I'd stay out longer—half an hour or more—with happy buzzing like music in my head.

Celía, one of the girls at work said, just before New Year's, I been meaning to tell you, you are looking really terrific these days.

It was true.

I circled around the file cabinets all afternoon, putting things away, singing.

That night, after picking the kid up and dropping him and his cousin off with his grandma for a couple hours, I skipped grocery shopping and just went home. I changed into some sweaty old things and went outside into the wind and dark and I ran again, very sweet and happy and like music, the way I had that morning, running off and onto curbs, twisting around cars and garbage cans and people, I didn't care. I hummed and sang going back upstairs. Needa opened the door for me, mad.

"Where the fuck you been? I feel like I ain't got a lover these days."

"Oh you got one, honey. Whether you want one or not."

"What's that supposed to mean?"

"Whatever you want it to, girlfriend."

She moped around the rest of the evening, drank about a six-pack of Ballantine and fell asleep on the sofa. Later, I went to pick up the kid. Walking home he said how big he was getting, how he was gonna be in first grade next year, and how he could take gym and run in the school track meet next spring.

That's good, I told him, it's good to have a plan.

We ordered pizza, watched TV, and drank Coca-Cola while Needa snored away on the sofa. I was feeling different—lighter, happy-headed, and full of fresh cold air from running again, but at the same time dark and warm inside. I put the kid to bed and left a kitchen light on for Needa, then turned in myself, breathing full and deep, sniffing camphor, mint, letting some calm clean-burning soft red feeling wash over me, droop my eyelids shut, wrap me up all safe and bright, and soon I dreamed.

In the dream I was running on dirt and grass through trees near the reservoir in Central Park—quick, effortless, light, my toes and ankles bouncing and strong—and next to me a man was running, and we breathed in perfect rhythm. I looked over. It was Salazar.

Alberto, I said, I want to run the marathon.

Listen to me, Celía, he said, you're not ready yet. You gotta do some shorter races first.

Okay, I said.

Then we stopped running.

He faced me, hands on hips, fierce dark-flame face, slender and serious and young. I noticed he wore a collar of beads, scarlet-wine red and white. Oh, I laughed, I thought so. You really are a child of Chango. So am I.

It's fire, Celía, he said. But everyone has a power. Use it for running. Use it for loving. Use it for God.

I woke up smelling rotten beer breath. Needa was sitting slumped over, head in hands on my side of the bed, crying.

"What is it, honey?"

"Lost," she sobbed. "I got lost."

I put my arms around her. Her cheeks were all soft and smelly, but there was that nice odor to her too, one it seemed like I remembered from long, long ago, woman smell, soap smell, a crumply warm feel of her hair and clothes.

Lost, she sobbed.

No, honey, I told her, holding her, rocking the both of us back and forth. No, honey, no, sweet woman, my Needa, don't you cry. You didn't get lost, you been found.

Help me, Celía, she said. Help me, God. Gotta work harder, keep up with you. I am so ashamed of my life.

I remembered the dream. I pulled her down alongside me on the bed, held her, rocking, whispering true things to the back of her neck. Telling how I was proud of her, and of our child, and our home. How hard we had worked. How far we had come. How, before taking on the whole rest of our lives, we had to do the small, obvious, necessary tasks, one step at a time.

"Like how I'm not gonna just jump in and run the marathon right off, honey. I gotta do some shorter races first."

"Huh," she sniffed, "get you, the expert. Who you think you been talking to, the angels?"

But she pulled my arms tighter around her when she said that, and I didn't want to fight, or let her go.

It happened like this: No more booze. No more videos. No more shit food.

I shifted the force of the power to purifying myself, for real. And, like magic, once I did that, Needa and the kid came around. Maybe one or both of them would make barf sounds whenever I dished up some brown rice stuff for dinner. But Needa's belly flab was shrinking, and she even started going after work, a few times each week, to pump iron with her buddies at some old gym. Those nights she came back fresh from the shower, cold air in her face, smelling of powder with a warm skin glow. Have to keep up with the little lady, she said, but in my own way, love, understand? I mean, running, racing, turning into some skinny fag, that is not your Needa's style.

End of May, I was going to run the Women's Mini-Marathon in Central Park, a little more than six miles. I laid down the law at home. No fucking up and no messing up between now and then. Cold weather, then warm, and warmer, rains and damp hot sunlight and hazy mist started floating past, through us, like we were nothing but thin vessels that for a moment could catch a whiff of the breeze and the universe, then lose it, let it go. I kept running, every day. The kid did okay in school. Needa and I started making love again some nights, oh, so nice, rubbing back and forth. Oh, so nice, to feel her touch around inside me again.

And then, late spring.

How it was the night before: I'm sitting around, we had some buckwheat noodles with vegetables for dinner, everybody's quiet, no TV, thinking about how I'm gonna run the race tomorrow with about nine thousand other women, and how they, the family, they have got to cheer us and watch, and I look at Needa and the kid and see how slender they are now, and healthy, how beautiful and handsome and slender, and start thinking how much they are mine—just that, they are mine. And I look down at my own bare feet and see that they are skinny, too. Bumpy with callouses and with veins. Bashed a little bloody around the big-toe edges. The littlest toenail on my left foot is dead and black. All from running through the mornings and the nights. From running in my dreams. We got changed, poof. Just like that. Thought we were gonna change ourselves, maybe even the world. But, poof, the world changed us. Through work, love, sacrifice.

Holy, I thought. This is holy.

I chewed cinnamon sticks for dessert the way Madrita recommended, went to sleep with a hint of fire inside.

I got up scared, scared in the morning. Too scared to notice how Needa was being so sweet, feeding the kid, making sure I drank water because it was looking to be a hot, hot day, pinning my racing number on my T-shirt straight with safety pins. #6489-OPEN. Too scared to notice we were leaving—leaving our home, taking the subway, walking, silent, through the heat of the morning.

Finally we made it, to the West Side, into the park. To hear music play over loudspeakers. Announcements blaring, half heard.

Reminders about some awards ceremony later, on a lawn. The lawn. Some lawn. To hot bright light crystallized through the trees, sunlight, damp blazing air, water stacked in paper cups on tables, and tables, and the laughing crying voices like in my childhood, so many people. A banner, a big blinking magic electronic clock, zeroed out, waiting. And runners, waiting: women, all shapes and sizes and ages and colors, thousands of them, of us, just thousands.

Baby, says Needa, I'm proud of you.

The kid's made friends already. Some other woman's twin sons, about his age. I catch sight of him, out of the corner of an eye, his half-smiling half-serious little handsome face, glowing under the rim of a baseball cap. Yeah, he's telling them, my mom's fast, too. My mom's gonna run the race. Me and my other mom's gonna watch.

Some things are forever inside us. Some things cannot get said.

That's why, when the gun went off, it was like this piece of me fell deep, deep down inside, into the dark well of myself— this was the piece of me that recorded, in absolute detail, every moment of the race—and lodged there, safe but never recoverable, at least not in words.

I can say that the different-colored crowd of thousands moved in a big shuffle at first, all together. Then, little by little, began to unbind into space, like it was some light-stitched vast fabric coming apart at the seams. So that at the start we were all the same, then some of us swayed forward, some back, some to one side or another, and the tarred hot surface of the road melted uphill into trees, green, brown, into a hot, misty, blasting summer air running blue and gray and yellow under sunlight. I can say that my heart popped right into the base of my throat and stayed there for the first mile so that I staggered along, sweating after only a few yards, gasping to breathe. Then something inside me let up—or gave up, yes—and my heart settled down into my chest where it belonged. I was sweating and suffering but could breathe again, and the elbows and bouncing breasts and shoulders and hair and flesh of women was all around me, smells of bodies and of the city and the trees and sun, and I drank water from somebody's paper cup, kept running, tossed it like a leaf to the cup-littered ground. I can say that in the second mile, once in a while, sweating and running, avoiding veering hips and limbs, I saw some girl go by with a Sony Walkman, wearing sunglasses with mirrored lenses, closed off to the world. Once in a while, too, conversation filtered into the sponging, soaking, deep-down fallen-off piece of me, women's voices in English and in Spanish and in other languages, too, trying to laugh, muttering encouragement. But by the third mile, fact is, there was not anyone chatting.

What there was was the breathing. Hard and uneven, or measured, controlled. I kept the feet plodding slow, steady, like the pace I did each morning, the pace I did some nights—but never as fast and light and easy as my dreams. Still, it moved me forward. Clumsy. Slow. With a little fat bobbling, yet, around hips and belly and thighs. Near me, all shapes. Like crazy soldiers in some war. The sweat gushed down me. It was hotter than I'd thought.

At each mile you heard them, calling out the time. Time? Time? I never thought of it before. How much it took to do one mile, or one block, or twenty. Each morning, some evenings, even in my dreams, I ran by the minutes. Thirty-five, thirty-six minutes. Into the fourth mile. Now it was feeling like forever. Now it was feeling like one more hill would be the last. My fat, bouncing thighs and sweating, gushing body would never be things of beauty like maybe in foolish moments I'd imagined; and maybe in my stupid dreams I talked about marathons— but here, here was a little stupid miniature marathon, and it hurt so bad I could not even imagine doing this again, much less running anything longer.

Then more water, more flesh around me, slipping on paper cups in my flopping old tennis shoes with this number safety-pinned right under my tits, over flabbing belly, every slight upgrade of road sending sunlight searing through me, stabbing thighs and ankles, making me gasp and hurt and, without killing myself, I ran as fast as I could. Clumsy. Fat. Slow. My heart settled back down, pounding with breaths, with mint and cinnamon and camphor. Sunlight shot through the leaves of trees. Hose spray cooled our skin, drenched our socks. More sunlight shot through, blinded me. Fire, I thought. For your husband, your child, your God. To hell with that, Celía. For your own living self. Okay, man, fuck everything. Fuck the whole sunlit sweat-smelling cinnamon-smelling fucking shark-circling world. Whiff of Chango. Fire in the belly. Fuck even your world of dreams. Because this, sweetheart, this—here—is real.

Then, for a mile, I knew what was real. All this, steeped in miserable sweat and sacrifice. I knew it without knowledge of the mind, only the sure undying knowledge of the body that can run and love, give birth, sob, suffer. And knowing what was real, and that this, this was it, now, only this, and it was enough, and that I lived now, really lived, and knew now what it was to breathe—knowing this, blind with pain, sweating and gasping and almost dead, I stared down and saw that there was a little hole in the tip of my right tennis shoe, near the little toe. It had rubbed the toe raw and, around the hole, the dirty white fabric was soaking through with blood. Then I felt all the dried-up pieces of me come to life and, suffering, I ran on the breath of the wind. Until, after a while, the wind deserted me. Just before six miles. Left me, one faulty woman, in a mob of suffering, moving flesh, to finish the last few hundred yards alone. It was all uphill. There were people watching, and I was ashamed, people screaming around me, I was running so slow, nearly dead of exhaustion and of shame, stomach in spasms, drenched with sweat, crying. Until I heard someone yell out Mom with a voice, among all the other little voices, meant only for me. And I heard Needa, laughing, crying, yelling, and heard that her voice was hoarse, a croak, almost gone: *Attagirl baby! My baby! My lady! You can do it youcandoityoucandoityoucandoit! Break an hour breakanhourbreakanhourbreakanhour!*

Fifty-nine minutes and fifty-nine seconds. But I was not lost, and I was not last.

Girlfriend, I said, get some pride.

I did.

Then I staggered under the big, heartless, blinking clock, the yellow sun, dripping water, my shoe spraying blood.

I got a medal. They gave everyone medals. Slipped around your neck, in the finishing chutes crowded with beaten, grinning women, a silvery goldlike medal on a red-and-blue ribbon, just for finishing. Then they gave you a carton of Gatorade. A free Mars Bar. And a plastic egg-shaped container full of mesh tan panty hose.

Needa hugged me. So did the kid.

They were all over me, screaming, proud and happy.

Runners were still finishing, running, staggering, walking. I moved through the crowds. I lay on the grass. Closed my eyes, with Needa sitting on one side and the kid on the other, each holding a hand, and I fell down into the deepest blasted-off piece of me that had come apart and wedged inside with the explosion of the starting gun, that would never, ever be the same. It was so dark, falling deep down there, full of iron and of water, musty brown and wet wet green and the still, malignant air; but also, it was red like blood, and bright, and filled with a bubbling, smoldering, surprising color. It was filled with this work and this imperfect love, and with chicken gizzards, sacrifice, camphor oil, rainbow light.

Something blared over a loudspeaker.

"And now...a special treat for all you ladies! To present the awards, we have with us here—"

I fell into a place of half dream, half sleep.

Needa poked my ribs.

"There he is, Celía. There."

Who?

"Your Salazar."

I turned my head in the grass. Salt was full in my sweat. Salt on my lips. I licked at it with the air and it tasted real, good, sweet. Opened my eyes to see the young, slender, serious man standing above me, body and clothes of a runner, his eyes in shadow, fierce face gazing down.

He nodded. Saying softly, politely, Good for you, Celía.

Alberto, I said, can I stop now?

No, Celía. He said it gently. Then he smiled. Not until you die. And even then—who knows?

I opened my eyes.

There was an awards podium, in the sun on the grass. Women, slender and beautiful, gifted young magnificent runners, walking up when their names were called over fuzzy loudspeakers, accepting the bright gold and silver statues they gave for awards. And there, with famous men and women athletes and politicians behind the podium on the stage in the sun and the park, there he was, handing out each statue, shaking each woman's hand. Salazar. There was no collar around his neck, no red and white of gods or saints of fire as in my dream. Not running, he seemed different. Quiet. Humbly human. Pale and young, and far away.

I started to cry.

Needa held me in her arms.

The kid crawled into my lap, laid his soft little cheek against my drenched, floppy chest.

"What is it, sweet?"

"It don't stop, Needa."

"No, my love."

"I gotta do some more of these."

"Okay, baby."

"And then, in a few years I think, I gotta do the marathon."

*Yes!* Alberto muttered, through a microphone, and shook some woman's hand. I squeezed the hand of Needa, and of our child. The fire kissed me.

*(1992)*

# Takanakapsaluk

*for Dr. April Martin*

I live here with another woman and our children, apart from the village. Deep in snow, made of snow, our home. In the winters we eat seal. We crawl under skins of bears, press close around the center pit of wood and rock and fire, bring the yapping dogs inside. We toss them bits of blubber.

In summers our home is elk hide, wolf hide. The dogs wrestle, play with sticks and shells in the grass. Our children grow taller, fly feathers in the breeze. We hunt, dry strips of fresh kill by the fire, spear fish in running streams and crush their flopping heads on rock, with flint knives gut out the bone. From the village men approach fearfully. A circle of wood and stone surrounds our camp. They're careful to remain outside.

Full of hate and terror, their eyes cast down, they say: *Here strange one, powerful one, wretched one, woman-child, Takanakapsaluk. Here, take this food, for your woman and your children.*

Based on an Inuit myth

Then they throw meat wrapped in sealskin to the center of the circle. Sometimes there are baskets, too, of dried roots and berries. And backing away, they retreat.

They never stay here long.

In their homes, in the village, whispering quietly among themselves they'll say: *It's done. Gifts for winter, given to the wretched one. May our winter game be plentiful. May our mothers not miscarry. May we never need her service. May her strange eyes never touch us.*

But again the days end early. Winter comes. When winter stays too long, the darkness screams with wind and dying animals. In our home of snow, deep in snow, the woman and our children and I curl close under bearskins with the dogs. We eat rotting seal fat. Breathe silently together around a fire pit in the storm. And with us, all is well.

But in the village, if the snows remain, the meat is gone and fires burn low. Outside, starving dogs gnaw flesh from their paws, perish footless, whining, turned to ice and bone. On lakes, the air holes freeze. Seals drown. And wolves go hungry.

Then into our circle, through the iced-over hides and furs and blocks of hardened snow, come the men of the village. They crouch before us. Raise their ravenous arms. With eyes staring down they plead: *The snows increase. There is no game to kill. And dogs die hungry in the dark. Our mothers miscarry. Our children perish. Please help us now, help us—strange one, powerful one, woman-child, Takanakapsaluk.*

I rise from dead bearskins, from flesh and living dog fur, from the arms of my woman and our children. I sigh. Chant good-bye to the fire. Bow my head, and reach. Trembling, the village men touch my fingerless hands. And we leave, together, in the darkness and the cold. Through ice storms. Blinding winds. Through all the death of winter.

I always go when they call.

Skin drums beat with bones in a snow home deep in snow

in the center of their village. I chew dried plants and dance, build a fire to call them here, all the scoffers and transgressors. Naked I dance, herbs run from my mouth, and the dance becomes a dream. They gather, afraid, hands shielding their eyes. Singing and sobbing: *See, see, how we have been foolish and wasteful, cruel and remiss, so it has come to this. Oh help us, strange one, strong one, fingerless one, woman-child, Takanakapsaluk!* Then they hand me their gift. Saying: *Go, Takanakapsaluk. Give this to the elk and seals and bears. Ask for their forgiveness. Beg for their return.*

Foam slides down the throat. My bare feet jump to bones and drums, the rhythm of their sobs and the wind. They fling me from their boat in the naked dream dance. I clutch at its sides, hanging on just for life. With flint knives they kneel, blades poised above grasping hands. They cut off all of my fingers. I scream, I dream, and the dream continues, dancing. Into the round of the air hole, woman hole, I fall, into pitiless water and earth. My eyes stars. My feet sun and moon. My woman hole the world. I go down to the center of the ice.

There it's warm, red and green. There are all the grandmother grandfather fishes and animals: elk, wolf, hare, seal and fox and bear. They gather around. Lick at my bloody finger stumps. Saying: *See, they have done this to you, too, woman-child, abused one, friend of beasts, Takanakapsaluk! For this they must be punished. We'll offer ourselves no more.*

"Sisters and brothers," I say, "do not keep yourselves from them. Without you, they starve. Their mothers miscarry. Their children are cold."

And with shaking, bloody, fingerless hands, I set the gift before them, unwrap it from white fur. Inside a mass of flesh and blood: entrails, tiny unopened eyes, nose, the beginnings of mouth and ears. Tender, bloody, half-formed tissue of an infant born too soon. They crowd around, clicking teeth. Mouths dive for the soft, soft flesh, and in this warm red-and-green still place at the heart of the earth and the ice now there are snapping, snarling, crunching sounds. In a small time the body is gone. Nothing remains but fur-shrouded streaks of drying red. The teeth and tongues wipe it furiously away.

Then they sit back, bellies full, licking their bloody mouths. And say: *Sing for us, Takanakapsaluk, sing!*

Delirious, ruined hands lifted in agony, I sing. Bleed. I sing for their forgiveness.

Later, wrapped in fresh furs by a fire, I sleep. In the center of the village, in the dying world of men. I wake, am sick, and drink snow. Sleep again, and dream the dreams of animals.

When I wake the storms have gone, winds ceased, and an unbroken blanket of snow sparkles quietly under nighttime stars. Hungry faces of villagers surround me. Saying: *How are the animals? What did they reply? What things did you see, Takanakapsaluk, at the center of the world?*

"They are angry. Yet accept your gift. And promise to return one last time. Still, you must atone. Avoid cruelty and waste. Then they'll forgive you. And then so will I."

They promise to do better. They always do.

They wrap me in new furs, new soft cloths for my terrible hands. Accompany me on the way back, outside the village, with gifts—fish strips, seal fat, food for dogs, wood for my woman and our children.

In our home deep in snow I rest, at the center of the world. Know that they will come again, pleading. And again, I will go. Yes this one final time.

Summer comes, daylight, the animals return. Our dogs are fat and happy. My woman beats fresh bearskin against rocks, scraping off dried brown matter with a fishbone, and our children grow taller.

The girl-child's time is almost come. When blood will run from her like a wound, and the villagers mutter of infants stillborn. Then she might fall ill one day, and be dragged off by frightened, angry men, in a feverish dancing dream, to some dark winter hole in the ice. *Go down,* they'll tell her, *strange one, friend of beasts, down into the ice carrying gifts. Go down to the center of the world. And save us. And return.*

She'll wake sobbing, her hands mere stumps of fingers. "Woman-child," I'll tell her later, cleansing the cloth that wraps her wounds, "pity them. Avoid them. Prepare your own skins. Feed your own dogs. Tend your own fire. Forgive your own desire. But always go when they call. And tend the fire in them."

*(1987)*

# La Bruja

Over the years I'd see her sometimes, red lips, whiff of perfume, sweat on fur, smelling Marlboros and Rémy and Coke and with sometimes-flashing, sometimes-softening eyes she'd slice a path through all those dykes to the bar. Brought the night air in. Everybody looked. But Labruja, just like royalty—she looked at no one. Then she'd sit. Her first drink always on the house.

Watching her, the steely-shelled dark wanting deep down in me tingled every time. Along with that pull—in the hands, in the hips. Go, it said, go to her. Not that I'd dare. The fact is I was too young, too broke, too stupid. Too soft. Soft butch. Yes. Truth is the thing you never admit.

But someone older, tougher, wiser, handsome and hard like stone, dressed fine with a good tie and polished shoes and a fierce face, would appear to light her cigarette. There were still some of them around—I mean they never really left—dykes you didn't fuck with. She'd barely touch the lighter-holding hand.

Then I would feel it drop around them both: a shining

glass bubble, magnet of hearts and cunts, sealing them off from the world.

I grew. Life was not kind. Sometimes it stabbed me bad and I'd wish for the courage to die, or to kill. In the middle of despair came these dreams of Labruja. Just this picture I kept in my head of her: a walking thing of high-femme glory that no pain of the world could touch or beat out of me. All this, and I'd never even spoken to her. Yet imagined her every day. And that, just that, was a reason to go on.

Meanwhile real life happened. I got older, smarter. Had some women and affairs. Learned how to be: how to treat women right, how to worship their hair and full painted lips. And then, later on, how to mess both up real good. Grease in your comb, on the sheets. A couple times I even fell in love—got my heart smashed, and smashed up some others. But one night after work I was having a beer and whooosh, the bar door opened to wind, burning ashes, and someone slinking by—Labruja. This time I caught her eye. That glance made me shake. And I noticed I was standing, foamy beer all over the table.

Petie yanked my jacket. "Where you think *you're* going? Child, better watch out for that witchy witch. She's high femme, high *drama,* burn you up and break you. Okay, you been warned."

By now, though, Labruja had looked away. Schlitz dripped down on my trousers, and all my friends were laughing. I shoved through elbows and thighs to find some place more quiet. No one was fighting or kissing in the stairwell, but it smelled like piss. I let the sour dark cool off my sweat. Sometimes, there just aren't enough corners.

Got out of the bar habit and stopped going much. But one Pride Day in June, after marching and parading and pretending to die with all the fags near that church, I went to some block party downtown. I was covered with sun and dust. Sleeveless

T, black jeans. I'd been working out a lot and felt good, and some pretty girls were looking. There were speakers like rocket launchers set up, everyone busy bumping with everyone else to the drum-beat blare. It was twilight. And across the street, moving slowly in an invisible circle all her own, was Labruja. Dancing. She wore a flowery light-print dress. Not as much makeup. She'd put on weight, too, so her hips were round, breasts pressed out against cloth flowers with soft fullness, and as I pushed my way over closer I could see her skin was tight and clear, the lips full red like a heart. She'd almost lost that ragged raw edge I remembered, looked like she was out of the life. The music stopped. Speakers crackled over the musical boom. Between buildings the sky got darker. She twirled around once more, opened her eyes. Then saw me. And smiled. I reached without thinking, took her hand like a treasure so our palms sparked against each other's, and bent down to kiss it. "Labruja," I said, "you look beautiful."

Her eyes seemed dangerous for a second, then tender. "Oh, honey, *call* me."

Some big dyke like a *thing* stepped in: leather boots, harsh handsome face, pale bloody eyes stabbing rage. "Who're you?" she said, and spun me around to face her.

Scared me at first. Then I got it together, said to myself, Addy, you are not some fucking punk. And to her, "What's the matter?"

"The lady's with me, is what." She was big, and raw—harder, wiser, tougher than me—but in that second what I saw was that she was vulnerable, hurt by the world a lot worse than I, in a way nobody could ever fix. Usually in those situations I'd back off, be a buddy, say hey no harm intended. This time, though, her hurt fed my meanness. This time, too, was Labruja. Labruja of my dreams, getting hustled away from me now in someone else's big T-shirted arms.

So I shouted stuff after them I never otherwise would have: "Hey, you got a problem? Well fix it at home, bro. The lady looked at *me*." And I was still shouting while they disappeared past fire hydrants and cement into shadows, when a couple other dykes grabbed both my arms, saying Shut up kid, calm down, don't take it like this. Nice-looking kid like you, you'll get your own woman some day—Labruja's with Mick now, understand? She is Mick's. That's all.

More years passed. I got to feeling good in an older, grown-up way, and I was just about cock of the walk late one spring-time afternoon, stepping out of work early and down to the gym to lift hard, do sit-ups, biceps, get pumped, that nice rush and the so-fine scent and flesh swell after shower, after towel-down. Bag of wet sweats in one hand, I was on the street whis-tling, breeze in the air, my shoes very shined. Remembering this rumor someone had passed on to me the other night: *Now's your chance, sweets. Mick left the bitch!* Well, I was ready. Old enough. Tough enough. Handsome enough. Had a job. Paid my own way. No major fuck-ups, no, no more. Just one more fine stud bounc-ing down a breezy springtime city street, quarters in my palm, heading for the nearest pay phone. This time I'd do it. Call that Labruja. This time, she was mine.

First phone had the receiver ripped out. But I maintained what you'd call serenity. Another corner. Quarter went in and I was whistling, heart thumping, waiting and waiting but no dial tone. I banged it a couple times with my fist but nothing slid back. Now there was one quarter left. So I headed for another bunch of phones a block away, my mouth dry and sweat start-ing at the roots of my hair. This one had a dial tone. I put in the quarter, punched all the right buttons.

Then a woman—I'd seen her here and there at some places, maybe, only now she was walking with a little boy of about three—brushed past. The kid got in her way and she tripped, dropped two brown bags of groceries at my feet. A catsup bottle smashed, mayonnaise splattered—all over my shoes. The kid fell on his knees, and he was crying.

"Shit!" I yelled.

"Oh God, sorry!" she yelled, and started to cry, too. I let the receiver dangle, stooped to help with their fucking groceries. The kid was really screaming. She was sobbing something about how it's food or rent and what the fuck was she gonna do now. I helped her pick up bruised apples, a box of smashed eggs. Out on the Drive it was rush hour, major traffic tie-up. Cars waiting at exits spewed and honked. My breezy springtime city turned into a whirling circle of chaos and sound, and in the center of it I was helping some bitch and her brat pick up their ruined groceries while the receiver of my dreams dangled close by, and I was ignoring a phone call I'd waited my whole life to make.

Later I stood covered with foodstuffs. Pressed the phone to my ear. Hello I said, vacantly. Maybe Labruja had answered it before, but now it was dead. I set it quietly back on the hook.

Sometimes gentlemanhood takes over. I let it do that with this grocery bitch and kid. Wiped off cans and bottles. Crammed as much stuff as I could into my gym bag.

Here, I said dully, I'll help you home.

Gee, she sniffled, that'd be great.

I pulled out some gum and gave it to the kid to shut him up. He paused with it halfway to his mouth, stared tear-stained and imploring up at her.

"Go on, sweetheart, you could have it."

Her voice was tender.

He was soft brown like her, with somebody else's eyes.

We walked slowly as he toddled along chewing happily, away from park and Drive, shortcutting through the projects. Past a couple dumpsters, brick, concrete. She lived up some flights, and in the dim light when we paused on landings I saw that she was not beautiful really but sweet, with a shining on her cheeks and way down deep in the eyes that told me yes, she was kind.

Her place was a little cozy crazy bright hole, plant-littered, toy-littered, that sucked you right in and made you want to stay. I helped her unload crushed containers of food, watched as she put them away. Just as I was about to leave the kid had to go potty. I waited while she mopped up his rear end. He seemed happy now so I gave him another piece of gum.

"Take off your shoes," she said. "I'm real sorry, I will clean them."

She set my shoes on newspaper, pulled out a cloth and brush and buffer, black polish, rags. I sat on her sofa barefoot, watching. How she bent gently over those shoes, with humility and care. How her fingers were gentle and strong. The kid sat on my lap, just like that.

"He likes you." She offered up the shoes. Taking them I touched her wrist. Skin rubbed. Eyes met. "Hey," she said softly, "you wanna stay for dinner?"

"Okay," I told her.

But it was like I wasn't in charge of my own voice. Some ache inside of me spoke instead, a deep sore aching mixed with quiet calm mixed with a desire that I didn't even know I'd had, but I could feel without knowing somehow that here, in here— if I stayed—she might ease it.

So I stayed.

I never really left.

That was Rosa.

More years passed. Things with me, Rosa, and the kid were great. If we had problems, we'd work them through. I didn't have much to complain about. At night sometimes she'd just touch and pull me in, her femmeness and hunger washing over me with every move of her soft woman body. What I had with them gave me a warm strong solid core inside. But the warmth lived right next to a darkness. It was the other part of me, the part of dream and unquenchable desire: a hard persistent shadowy butch thing that left me always restless, always somehow far away from what I loved and had. I kept that part pretty quiet. Most times, didn't even touch on it myself. Things were too damn good.

One cold late winter in the middle of all this wonderfulness, the kid had vacation and she decided they gotta go to Miami and see his grandma. She and he will fly super-saver; four days later come back to me. I helped them pack. Kissed and hugged them good-bye. Put them on the bus to LaGuardia. Missed them.

"Yo," said Petie later that night, on the phone, "you heard?"

"Heard what?"

"Shit. Labruja. She's at St. Vincent's. She's dying."

"Whaddaya mean dying?"

"I mean like, *dying*. I mean I guess the life caught up with her."

I worked out hard at the gym. Picked up a video on my way home. In the kid's room I turned down his blanket, just so, the way I did every night, so that the bed was waiting for him— even though they wouldn't be back for days. I got to sleep around midnight. There were voices in my dream. *Child,* they said, *your heart is your own.*

Next morning was Saturday. I bathed and dressed, combed and polished to kill. Money in the pocket. And rubbers. I was packing, for the first time in years. The cock buckled on with leather sat there with its base above my cunt, the rest of it strapped back between thighs, a faint bulge swelling out against my baggy jeans crotch. It was unfamiliar for a minute or two, my walking clumsy, self-conscious, then I got the rhythm, then I had the power, power of a dream, power of a lover, and I walked outside so sure of dreams and of the realness and power of desire, for the first time in forever.

It was cold, streets and trees bare, the wind blowing garbage around an early weekend morning stuck in the winter chill
between snows. I stopped at the Korean guy's fruit stand and
stared at the roses. One stood alone, silvery soft naked, strange,
like shaped metal on fire.

"I'll take that one there."

"That platinum rose. Rare, only one left, ten bucks."

I didn't argue. Made sure he wrapped the stem and tied it
with white ribbon. Then, holding it close, I hailed a cab heading west.

St. Vincent's, I said, off of Seventh.

They gave me a pass at the desk. I was up elevators and
down halls, dodging wheelchairs and carts. Peeking around the
corner of a dark room. Thumping heart. Shy.

"Labruja. You remember me?"

She was propped on pillows, her makeup fresh. "Addy,
honey," she said smiling, "of course!" and offered a hand, very
gracious. I took it gently, turned it to kiss. Ran a finger over it
and could feel veins. I sat on the side of the bed and sensed for
a second the sharp knob of a knee against my back. She moved
it discreetly away with a faint swish of white sheet.

I noticed bouquets and vases of flowers, cards and presents
on the little table next to her bed. They were all pretty, all expensive, crowding each other out. Too many for the nightstand
to contain. Then I looked down at the single, dumb little rose
in my hand and felt small for a second, shabby, still too young
for her somehow. The lady had plenty of friends and admirers.
She hadn't exactly been waiting for me all these years. But I
offered it anyway.

"Here, every pretty girl deserves flowers."

This made it almost okay. Labruja held it to her cheek a
second. Then guided my chilled hand to her nose, mouth, and

cheek and breathed deep.

"God, you smell like outside! Like the air, I mean, like the world. Oh, it smells so good!"

"You can't die, Labruja," I blurted. "Because of women like you, I never killed myself." I sat back and apart then, my fingers suddenly clumsy without hers. Surprised because I had no idea that's what I felt or would say, but there, there it was, and it was true.

She gave a little gasp. And cried. The tears made mascara-edged rivers through rouge, powder, foundation. I dabbed at them with a hanky.

We talked some, quietly. Shyly at first. About her life. Mine. We'd never really spoken much before. Then she lay back on the pillows, very tired, and took my hand in hers again.

"I want to run away," she said, sadly, "but I can't."

Already an idea was ringing in my head. I reached through bouquets for the phone.

Yes you can, I said. Let me take you.

After the call I turned away while she dressed. I found her coat in a closet near the bed. It was long, long-sleeved, covered the hospital ID around her wrist. Then we were walking slowly, casually, around hallway carts and wheelchairs and trays of un-claimed lunch, through the antiseptic smell, avoiding nurses' eyes. And down. In a dream haze. And out—on the street, among cabs, in the cold. Tears came to her but didn't flow. A taxi stopped and I opened the door. Trembling, I helped her inside.

"Uptown," I said. "To the Waldorf Astoria."

Rich people's hotel lobbies are all carpets and glass, lights, terra cotta, gold, and everyone bustling silently. No they are not silent but muffled, muted, their voices refined and footsteps hushed. So that's how it was: the whole big rich unfamiliar place surrounded me and her but we moved forward through it in the same warm protective bubble that had carried us this far. I sat her down on a chair.

Petie met me, eyes darting everywhere, all done up in his uniform of wine-scarlet with bright gold tassles. The little hat brim over his face, sort of ridiculous, and at the same time all business. He spoke without looking at me, nervous, and handed over the keys.

"Twelfth floor, number 1285. You got until noon tomorrow. Then the next shift comes on and it's scheduled to clean." His voice had gone husky, there was stubble on both cheeks. I figured he was on the juice again. Personally, I wouldn't touch that stuff, but it was none of my business anyway.

Thanks, I muttered, sweating.

And keys in hand, I floated across the carpet like I belonged there with all the muffled, smart-dressed servants and guests, to the soft, plush lobby chair where Labruja sat next to a mound of someone else's high-polished leather luggage, pale and waiting, half a smile on her lips. I offered my arm. Very gentlemanly. And together we traveled to the row of silently blinking elevator buttons. Out of the sides of their eyes people glanced at us sometimes, glanced again, seemed puzzled, turned heads ever so slightly to stare in that discreet don't-ask way of the wealthy and polite. Something in the eyes turned hard and self-satisfied once they'd seen that yes, we both were women, and no, we could not fool them. Poor straights. They'd be disappointed if they'd known that I didn't even want to—fool them, that is. I was too far away from their life to try, and the woman on my arm took me farther. So we waited, Labruja and I, and we floated up together noiselessly in the glass-shining, brass-shining elevator. Down hallways with carpets that absorbed our feet. Where the lighting was delicate, kind on her exhausted face and eyes. Where the shake of her hand and the flush of her fever was hidden, known only to me now, and I held the shake of her and the flush of her in my own hands and heart.

Labruja, I said. Just that—her name.

And opened the door.

Silent flick of a light switch. The carpets, smooth walls, sparkling polish of things. Plush sofa and chairs. Gilt-edged mirror. Heavy thick drapes to pull across windows sparkling out on city skyline. A little pint-sized refrigerator stocked with snacks wrapped in pretty French and English packages. A bar with every kind of fancy booze under the sun. All these things were there for us. Maybe Petie'd kill me later, but I had to try stuff out. Poured spring water for the lady—she couldn't stomach anything else, she said—and popped a soda can for me. Sure I thought about champagne. But Labruja wasn't drinking hard stuff, not any more. I decided maybe I wouldn't either.

She was like a kid for a while, asking me to bring her things to look at: the room service menus, the special thick glossy entertainment magazines. Me? I was a willing servant. In between doing what she bid, bringing hotel knickknacks to her, taking them back to their places, I sat next to her on the sofa fingering velveteen and cushions, and we talked. We talked the afternoon away. Flicked on the TV—cable—with a multipurpose smooth-buttoned remote. There'd been a scent to her when we came in, I realized. Hospital disinfectant, alcohol swabs, very medicinal. Now, though, it was gone. She turned the TV off. Talked some more, this time about Mick. The first thing that brought them together, she said: Mick was strong.

I didn't know whether to believe her or not.

"I want to feel someone strong again," she said. "I think I'd like to feel you that way, strong and alive."

I'd only been waiting my entire life.

I leaned over closer to her heat and fever. Then I just pulled her up and onto me. Her legs and arms wrapped around, riding.

I rested against a wall, holding her. She was frail, child-light, so easily supported. I moved my hands on her ass and thighs slow, pressing her down, moved my hips up into pure woman smell and nylon. That's when she felt it for the first time, and breathed out once, loud, surprised, "*God,* hon'."

The bed was king-size, pillow-littered, a vast thing to get lost on. I rolled over it into her mouth and hair. She pressed fingernails against my neck. Then something fierce got me moving on top of her so hard and blurred and fast I forgot who I was, and pulled back for a moment, blinking, when she called out in pain. She made one great effort then, pushed me down by the shoulders. Crawled on top of me, very graceful, older, wiser, knowing and smiling, rubbing against my thighs and belt.

"Stay still, hon'." She pushed off my jacket. Unbuttoned my shirt, pulled the tails of it out to each side, unbuckled my belt and teased down a zipper, then briefs, then reached between my legs and the cock sprang rubbery free.

"Mmmm-mmmm. That for me?"

"Yes, baby."

"Well," she said, "I got a present for you, too." She went into one of my pockets and pulled out a rubber, and the plastic wrapping crackled. I reached. "Uh-uh," she said, "let me." With one expert motion it was on, little waiting bubble at the tip for a sperm that does not exist except in the hard strong make-believe love-fucking of the mind. She rolled to one side and peeled her nylons off. Then crouched over me again in nothing but the dress, and came down on top of me, slowly, while I guided the cock inside.

"Aaah," she sobbed, hurting, and took it all in. Then just sat on it and on me breathing fast, tears streaming. I reached up under soft flaps of dress to hold her hips. Ran my thumbs across her belly, across all the bumps of scars.

"They cut everything out of me, hon'."

I licked one finger, touched it to her clit, and she moaned. "Not everything."

"Be soft, hon'," she said. "Go slow."

I rocked up into her with a sure, smooth motion that made her lips part and eyes flick shut, then open, made her smile

sweet. It was something that in my daydreams I always meant
for her to feel. Meant for her to know just who and what I
could be for her here, in this room, in this place, in the shadows, just for her: a lover who knew how to wait, and knew how
to move, to hold back, give, fuck, caress, take, a woman who
was old enough and ready enough, tough enough, soft enough,
wise enough now, and in love. Who had come to find her still
alive—finally, yes, and not a moment too late.

Sometime during that afternoon we had all our clothes
off, strewn over floor and bedcovers like unnecessary things,
and in the heavy, peaceful curtain-drawn quiet lay side by side
on damp sheets, half asleep. I was totally naked, not even packing. She ran a hand in circles on my belly.

"So smooth. Mine's ruined."

"No, baby."

"Mick never let me touch her."

"Hmmm. But you wanted to?"

"Oh," she mumbled, suddenly shy, "yeah. Sometimes.
What about you with your lady? You let her touch you?"

"Well, sure, sometimes."

"You *soft*," she teased. Then, very serious, "See, stay that
way. Stay nice and strong and soft for your lady. Stay good to
her."

Then she slid a finger inside me without even asking, and
something escaped from my mouth, a piece of my guts, like a
breath or a sound. What all the surgery had left criss-crossed
her belly, a dark red death messenger. Platinum petals. But the
rest of her was still alive, her hands and eyes seeking life.

"You just *let* me," she whispered fiercely. "Stay right there,
like so. Give it to me. Give it to me. Give it to me, honey."

I showered in a bathroom like a palace. Later I cleared
marble shelves of all the special little containers of shampoos
and conditioners and stuffed them into a bag.

When I drifted out with the steam she was dressed. Feverish, weaker than ever, but sitting there in the quiet-draped dark
smiling. She hadn't bathed. "I want to smell like today," she
said, "for as long as possible."

I left the key and a ten on the dresser. Big spender. But in
the elevator all that floating peace inside started to be pulled
down, pushed apart, like shattered glass, ruined light. Grace
and mercy left me. I had no idea what time it was. Stepping out
into the cold of a bitter winter weekend night told me it was
late, and my insides went desolate. A cab stopped and the hotel
hop opened a door for Labruja. I gave him a couple bucks.
Watching her fold herself slowly, achingly inside, I knew for
sure then how weak she was, how little time she had, so when I
climbed in after her I sent all the bad fear feelings inside me
away and pressed her hands between mine. St. Vincent's, I told
the guy, downtown, take Seventh. And please take it easy, the
lady doesn't feel good.

I'm sorry, he said, no problem.

Shampoos rattled in her purse.

"Should I call you?" I whispered.

"No, I don't think so, hon'."

We were silent. But partway downtown in that cab on that
night-lit city avenue we turned to each other, suddenly laughing. Roaring. It came from deep in the gut, warm, delicious,
spiced like life. I understood then that this was the last time I'd
ever see her, my desire and dream, my Labruja. Because somehow she was mine. Oh, sure, maybe other people's, too. But
also *mine* in a way that she'd never been before. And as long as I
lived—which, for sure, would be longer than she did—I could
have her this way.

At the hospital's main entrance we were both still smiling.
I got out to open her door. She staggered by, utterly exhausted,
but with a fiery look to her, brushed my cheek with her lips. I
watched her walk unsteadily away. She waved once without turning. Last I saw she'd taken out the platinum rose, which was

wilted with cold and crushed, but she was holding it to her nose breathing deep. She was entering the lobby, her patient wristband showing from beneath a coat sleeve. She turned once to blow me a kiss. Then entered the revolving door of shadows and of glass, dancing, reeling on feverish feet, spinning round and around.

A couple days later Rosa and the kid came back. I met them at LaGuardia. We went home together in the bus.

The kid was happy because he got some toys and shit from his cousins. Rosa looked great. Said it was good to see everyone but she'd missed me. Yeah, I said, I missed you too. Then she was quiet.

That night we fixed spaghetti with meatballs. I made tomato sauce from scratch. The kid helped, stirring in onions. And our whole place got that warm home family air, covering us all in a kind of blanket of closeness, familiarity, and affection. We ate, caught a couple shows on TV. Bathed the kid, tucked him into bed, and it was my turn to read a story. Later I headed for the kitchen to help clean up and found myself drying dishes.

"Coffee?" Rosa took out the can. I said sure.

"Tried calling you the other night," she said. "You weren't home."

"Huh," I mumbled, "which night?"

"Oh," she said, "the one before last."

I was glad she couldn't see me. But gentlemanhood kicked in fast and helped me save my sorry butt. I stayed right on my toes. "Oh," I said, very casual, "that. Well, I was pretty beat, baby. I just turned in early, must of turned off the phone."

"Ah."

Soon the coffee was bubbling away, filling the warm kitchen with a homey, fine perfume.

"You know," she said, "Angie called the day before I left.

She told me something about that ho, you know, the one used to go with Mick? Well, she said the bitch is dying."

"Uh-huh," I said. "No kidding?"

Then before I knew it an almost-full can of El Pico came sailing through the air, bounced off the kitchen cabinet leaving a big scarry dent in wood, just about an inch above my head. It crashed into the sink and I wheeled around to face her.

"What the fuck!"

Her face was burning, eyes and mouth anguished slits. "That," she hissed, "that's for turning off the phone."

I spent a few nights on the couch.

Winter slowed us down.

Springtime the kid was doing great at school, Rosa got back to her old sweet ways, I kept up pretty steady at the gym. Since that one night, no more coffee cans got tossed my way.

I heard through the grapevine that so-and-so was with so-and-so, and this one had left that one to go there—fucking dykes and their affairs, you know, all of us hopping around on this board of a city like a bunch of Chinese checkers. In my heart center settled that big sure steadiness again: Rosa, and me, and the kid.

Desire is one thing with a mind and a heart of its own. It picks us up, spins us around in the brilliant cloud world of extreme unction, crisis times, life and death, a soul-world of always-passion, gold hotels, and of dreams. Then it spits you out real good. Me? Like most folks, I move most times in the touchable, nondream, material world of real things: a job, a home, a woman and child. Just me. In all my soft butchness, hard womanness, all my heart's truth and lies. Nobody's savior. Nobody's angel.

Labruja died that spring. They had a service at the Community Center. I heard that Mick cried.

One afternoon weeks later I was lying near the window in our bedroom after work, waiting for Rosa and the kid to come home. A leaf blew past the fire escape riding on what looked like a puff of something thicker than air, like silver smoke. I saw it through the turned-up blinds. And I thought: Desire. Petals. Labruja.

My woman and kid, they are so *real.* Kindness. Anger. Love. What I need, for my life. And I am what they need, too. This I know, deep down inside.

But I've got this other desire inside for things that don't have a whole hell of a lot to do with the life that happens to me, to most of us I guess, day after day. Call it crazy butch dreaming—Petie does. The hard buried part. The not-woman, not-man, just-butch darkness in me. That could love and want Labruja.

See, she was real, too. Not what I needed—but what I *wanted.* What I almost never grew up enough for.

The leaf blew by. Puff of smoke. Lipstick trace. A dream. Lucky me. To get, in life, what I wanted. And to also give back something. And, no matter how many cans of El Pico go sailing past my head, to be smart enough to shut up about it.

Femmes. They're a mystery to me. Mine, or hers, or yours—oh, we think we're so tough, but none of us ever own them. Yet among them sometimes are the ones just looking at keeps your dreams alive, so you can go on surviving yourself. It's this passion they have for what you are in your own butch heart. It never dies in them—it's something you can count on. Keeps you going when you'd rather not. It caresses you free of shame. So no matter who you love in everyday life, you will never stop dreaming of them. Every living day. Gods or goddesses or demons give me this: my dream femmes, these special tender women whom you want without end but also somehow without selfishness. I mean, without coveting. See, women to me are love. Also, desire. But that's not all they are.

Alone, I'm mostly my own butch shadow. Watching the drift. Wanting the dream. Inside the shadow, desire rises. Then the magic. And love. All but unspoken. Says one word, one yearning, a name. Always and forever to me—Labruja.

Some women, you're glad they've lived. And not just for yourself.

*(1995)*

# The Piper

Spring was full of chilled rain that year, smog-heavy. The mushrooms were in bloom. I'd walked charred forests and marshland filled with bones. Then slogged along a muddy road with so many others and their sad carts and possessions, all of us heading for Hamlin. Artisans, mendicants. Quack doctors, barbers, penitents. Women and their children, hooded infants bosom-shrouded in the rain, fathers' brows beaded with effort of the pushing, the hauling, and the mud. Children clutching rudely carved toys. Children's eyes, children's smiles, fresh powder smell of innocence. I searched them out, I looked away. The long intermingling lines of people moved on, stumbled, slowed, and stopped, miles away from the city gates. So many wanted shelter. The gatekeepers, taking full advantage of war and plague, were busy exacting tolls. Behind them factory spires twisted out of smoke and I saw it then: the rat, a dark angel, red-eyed, teeth spiked and wings spread, suspended over the town, over the city of Hamlin.

Based on "The Pied Piper of Hamlin," a German folk tale

I took a job as deejay at the Mountain Club, where queers went at night. Everyone knew about the place.

When I say *everyone* I mean, of course, *us*—not straight people, not Hamlin at large. We queers knew. We danced there and caressed and had too much to drink in the dim corners, on the hot-lit Mountain dance floor every night. We lived day in and out for that era between midnight and 3:00 A.M., when everyone—our everyone—was there. To show up alone at that special time was to announce your availability. Bargains were made, liaisons begun. And black-market perfume became a riotous, urgent smell, rising with a mist of cigarette smoke and scotch in the strobe lights' flashing. The Mountain was special; not just anyone could walk through her doors. We wanted dykes hungry for power and surrender inside. And we wanted no straights. Spotting them was my specialty, hovering as I did in my booth above the dance floor. A lot of them did manage to get in, nonetheless, because they'd heard about the great dancing, the music, me. Or because they had a bet with someone, or were bored, curious, frustrated. I hated them even more than I hated the politicians and professors, even more than I had once hated rats, or the virulent plague itself.

But one—a delicate, young, exquisite little thing with long dark curls and wounded eyes—was the daughter of Hamlin's mayor. The mayor was law in Hamlin. We paid him off, through a series of designated emissaries, with a suitcase full of cash each month. A suitcase I delivered to the first in a chain of nameless goons packing guns. In return, the mayor let us alone. I noticed his daughter, of course; everyone did. She was so beautiful—we were all a little bit in love with her. I never dreamed she was in love herself.

Oh, and copious peddling of this or that was acceptable, even desirable. Did I forget to say that we provided Hamlin's straight residents with a great service, by absorbing much of the city's criminal element after hours? The discreet, commercial

criminal element, courtesy of the mayor: those with useful gifts
to barter or trade. The war staggered along as usual. The plague
was at its height. Politics had passed us by. We heard about it
now and then—politics, the war—and scoffed in a kind of
amazement. It was, in any case, all old news to us.

I played music. Women danced to it. One of those girls was
the daughter of the mayor. And me—I watched as she danced.

Perfume. Sweet, sweet sweat. There's a feeling to damp cloth,
to how a femme brushes her silk sleeve across your face, carrying away the wet. Cigarette tips soaked in wine, on a table. The
twisted metal cap to some lost poisonous bottle. A bracelet. Smell
of hair against a neck. All these sensations drifted through me
as I called the tune and watched women dance, until most nights
there was nothing else inside me at all except sensation and an
endless subliminal series of elusive memories. No real thought,
no grief.

When I'd first arrived in Hamlin, just one more ruined
refugee, things had been different. I'd stood at rigid, exhausting
attention all night looking over the crowd, contemplating my
injured life. But as time went on and the plague failed to touch
me, this tension was swept away by the continual breeze of sensation, nightly blasts of color and texture and smells, until I was
just exactly what I was—the Piper. No more, no less. Standing
there momentarily scrutinizing, or sitting back to watch everything pass by, and that was just fine.

The less timid always approached me. Not because I was
beautiful—I wasn't, not at all. But to some I seemed attractive
in a strange brooding way, and rumor said I did it right in bed.
Go figure. I understand little about how to judge or rate love
when it's purely physical; I partook of it so rarely. Out of choice.
It's hard to touch or feel through a plastic bag. To tell the truth,
when making love I'd never accept pleasure myself anyway—
prophylactic devices or no. It was touching another, having that

power over her, wanting her wanting me, picking out the rhythm I'd make her dance to, that thrilled me. But in order to feel that thrill, I required absolute infatuation—of myself as well—and the truth also is that most women failed to infatuate me. Making love from the top necessitates laborious planning sometimes. So much work; it was all such an elaborate routine. Without infatuation, why bother?

Eventually, my long stretches of chosen celibacy were accepted by the brothers as a sort of personality quirk, like a funny way of tying your shoes, of stabbing out a cigarette. And eventually I, too, was accepted as one of the less dispensable fixtures at the Mountain, along with the bouncers, the bartenders, and the regulars.

It was easy to forget the plague in there, easy to think that this basement space was the world: a world of women dancing and drinking and kissing under white-hot flashing lights. Because when you worked at the Mountain what you saw of life was pretty much contained within its walls—a cavernous converted cellar and first floor in an otherwise condemned neighborhood over on the West Side.

I got there by evening, worked until closing time, then stayed for free drinks. Maybe before six there'd be breakfast—coffee, dripping eggs on thin toast, and that foul, after-hours taste on the tongue—or maybe I'd skip food, take my pills, and begin the trip home. I walked crosstown often, especially in summer. That early there weren't many hearses. Just me. Just the rats. I'd feel sometimes as if the streets were my own private property. I'd jump off curbs, tread the white dividing lines on broken cement, while to the east smog sifted over the river, orange fires glowed in the burning parts of town, red sky dimmed to yellow then yellow-gray, the sun rose.

Home was some hellhole of a squat I'd claimed with force and ingenuity, my own private, sacred space: roach-infested, clogged pipes, multiple locks on doors and windows, steel bars and rusted metal alloy shutters entrenched in walls and sills against the continuous assaults of the homeless, the desperately addicted and ill, those who slept behind garbage cans nightly and tried to break in each lawless day. Home was dishes crusted in the sink, mail unopened, phone calls unanswered or desperately awaited, Black Talon bullets filling extra clips for the semi I carried everywhere. But most of all, home was just a bed—a soft, unmade bed to fall into. I'd keep steel bars and shutters closed, sleep the sunlight away. And when an alarm clock rattled me awake it was evening again, time for the Mountain.

I'd get out my pipe. I'd slip it through my belt. I'd throw on a shoulder holster, too, and the semi, some extra clips. Boots. Shirt. Suit and tie. The gun, the clothes, they were just for sheer survival. But the thing that gave me a calling, a name, was both a necessity and an extravagance. My pipe was tool and fetish. It was bold, bold delight. It meant that I aimed to please, that I didn't just play music—I ran the fuck, I led the dance.

"Where's that pipe?" bolder girls would ask, squeezing my trousers' crotch like a plea.

I loved those nights.

It was on such a night—during a break when I'd left a tape going and slow songs drifted from it, signaling a lull—that the daughter of Hamlin's mayor, that exquisite curiosity seeker, brushed up against me as I made my way through the crowd. Her eyes rounded with surprise. Looking into them for a second, I fell in love. I don't know why. Then I collected myself and winked, took her hand, led her through the gaggle of sweet-smelling, sweat-smelling bodies. She seemed willing. Her hand beat a pulse into mine, gentle, rhythmic. But just shy of the dance floor that hand began to shudder like the rest of her, and she pulled back. My guts churned. No, she mouthed into my ear, leaving a lipstick trace, *No, please, not yet.* I let her go. Then stepped just out of reach until she followed me along.

I pulled her to me. The tape segued into a slow, slow dance. Her arms went around my neck. For a while we moved together quietly; I could tell that she liked it.

Then I did something I hadn't intended. Midway into the slow, slow dance I reached down and pulled the back of her blouse until it fell out of the silk and leather that trapped it, cupped both my hands against the smooth, wet flesh underneath. I felt my hands moving with perfect grace somehow, etching deliberate circles on the naked small of her back. And I could feel my own thighs shaking into silk and cotton. Voltage went up my spine, buzzed around the back of my neck. I moved my lips and tongue on her ear, her dark curls covering my face until we stopped and swayed against each other. Something sweet buzzed, swooned, burned a blank over everything. I felt my head drop back like it had some pillow to rest on instead of just air, and the sweet thing spread, hot, colorless, then shot up and out the top of me. When the music changed we stood there pressed together, breathing.

*Sorry,* I said—and I was—but I didn't know why, or even if I'd said it out loud. I just knew that the power in me had fled. I was bereft of magic. Somehow, she had done that. Worse still, I wanted her to do it again.

I pushed her gently away, then headed for the door, bumping lots of elbows and breasts to get there. Moved outside and a gust of smoke blew with me. I could smell it on my hair, hands, the odor of ash on sweating cloth that stuck to my chest, a hint of death. There was another smell, too—something indefinable. I'd caught a whiff of it when her stray dark curls had brushed my neck: her perfume, mixed with whiskey. A rat scuttled across the tops of my shoes and vanished.

"Hey, you there. That's no way to be."

Smoke and dull lights spilled out the noisy door once more, got muffled when it closed with a thud. She stroked my arm and I let her, but when she pressed against me for a kiss I turned my own face away. Then held her firmly at arms' length. I'd felt her breasts and hard nipples through the shirt. They reminded me of the leftover quivering at my own core, reminded me of the fact that my legs were still shaking, and I didn't want her to see. Breeze blew from somewhere, bringing a scent of garbage. The alley wall held me up. Pull it together, Piper, I told myself. Regain control. Too many hours between now and dawn; you don't want any mistakes. But the girl looked injured.

"Oh, hey, why not?"

"Your daddy wouldn't like it." But we both knew that wasn't really it. The night air was cooling my flesh; I could seize a little control now. Instinct said to wait.

I watched her lips make words, but no sound came out: *Why not?*

In the shadows her face was disbelieving, then humiliated, her voice desolate.

"Please."

"Please what?"

"Don't go."

"Why? You like me or something?"

"Yes."

I eased my grip, let her wilted body closer. "Tell me how much. How much do you like me?"

I ran a hand along her neck, up her cheek, to the beginnings of tears on an eyelid. The lips moved again. *Please,* they said, silently. I traced them with a finger, smudged lipstick and tears away, brought the finger back to my own mouth to suck it. It occurred to me that if she carried plague we'd both die soon. For a moment I thought she would fall; she was shivering all over now, not fighting anymore. So I relaxed and let her lean forward against me, took her face between both hands and turned it up until the mouth opened, just so. Lips quivered as I teased them with my tongue, then they seemed to melt away like ice on a flame when I kissed them.

I let her hands stay against the backs of my thighs, let myself be pulled forward gently, rhythmically, then released, again and again. I played a game with her lips, holding them open with my fingers sometimes, sometimes only with my tongue. I was in control now, and it felt good. I'd become suddenly cold, full of clarity, of a boundless ability to plan and intuit. But I was still walking a narrow line between having all the power and losing it completely, and I knew it. I moved back away from her, plucked her hands off to hold them between my own. The dark eyes met mine fully—pained, wanting, afraid. I wondered what the fear was. An invitation? Rats whimpered in the darkness. I wondered how she'd slipped out of the mansion this time. I wondered if the mayor usually sent spies after her, and where they were right now.

"What do you think happens now?"

"Now? You...you—"

"I what?"

"Come home with me."

I laughed, softly. "Won't your daddy mind?"

"He's somewhere else. Until Wednesday."

"Busy guy. Somewhere else? Why'd you lie like that? There's nowhere else to go."

I passed a hand over her breasts. They were gorgeously soft under the barrier of cloth, nipples stiffened, aching to burst. Maybe it was a kind of pity that made me stop. That, or the thudding of my heart. I would touch them later, anyway, and when I did she'd be naked. But there was plenty of time between now and then. Plenty of time to dominate, control. Get back the power. Get back the music.

Gas was rationed; it mostly went to the hearses and politicians' cars. So we took a bike rickshaw all the way uptown. Passing through neighborhoods of withered prosperity, where garbage cans burned in the streets. Passing the last church left in Hamlin.

The minister was a fundamentalist sort who hated queers. He was always decrying us in the morning papers, accusing us of bringing plague to the city. He and his wife and children huddled together on steps in the rain as we passed. A mass of drenched, miserable, shivering refugees around them.

Hoarsely, he shouted, "Hallelujah!"

Shuttered windows turned blankly on them. The preacher's collar was frayed and gray. He wore dark-rimmed glasses with one of the lenses cracked; a thin strip of masking tape ran diagonally across it.

"And why, my friends, why have you come to Hamlin? What forces brought us here together, some of us starving, some of us lame, some of us tired, but all of us full of God's glory, to stand here, together, in this city, this last remaining outpost of civilization? I'll tell you, my friends!" He paused. Raindrops streamed across masking tape.

From the crowd came a shrill, "Tell us, brother!"

The preacher breathed in rain. "The forces that weave their ways among us, that bring us all here to stand together, my friends, in humanity's last place, these forces are the power of the Lord! The power of God to ordain and uphold, to avenge and lead the Sexually Righteous!"

"Amen!"

Our rickshaw clattered on.

The mayor and his daughter lived in one of Hamlin's last existing villas: a compound surrounded by high gates and barbed wire. She paid the driver well. Clutching coins, he coughed into both fists, and I wondered if he had flu or plague, wondered if he would live out the night, and if not, who would bury him. She opened the gates with a special remote. We walked past gardens, ponds and trees shrouded with light mist. It was a place of dark beauty, seemingly separate from the whole dirty city that surrounded it—quiet, flowering, an island of rural calm.

Then I saw the mayoral mansion, a vast fort of wood and stone set starkly in the rain.

A door slid open. She led me inside.

It was quite still. Somewhere, an ancient clock ticked. The floors were high-gloss walnut, the rug Persian antique. She pulled a cord and sashes flew across glass, obscured the empty sparkle of pool and patio; she pressed something on the wall and golden light rose dimly from each corner, aimed so that shadows played across expensive things placed everywhere. I stood at the carpet fringe. Six crystal brandy snifters waited on a bar.

"Would you like a drink?"

"No."

She turned once to smile—inviting, a little amused. Ran her hand along an armchair. It came away dustless.

"Have a seat."

I did. "Your parents like collecting things."

"Mommy's gone. The plague. She didn't like it—collecting things, I mean—not especially."

"Your father, then."

She shrugged. "His staffers, really. Daddy...well, he doesn't know the difference. He just pays lots of money to people who do. Get nice things, he tells them, make it look like the plague can't touch us here. Important people pay him to make sure everything outside stays just like it is. Everyone dying all the time. Dead people—they leave chairs and desks and beds, expensive things, and if the rest of their family's dead too, Daddy's men just go there and they bring stuff back. Or they sell it. They take a percentage. They bring the rest of the money here and they give it to Daddy. And he gives it to...to the important people."

"What about you? You like what they bring back?"

"No. It reminds me of death. I want to get out—"

"To go where?"

"The Mountain," she said. And laughed. Then poured good

burgundy into a snifter and sipped some. In the light it looked like ink, swimming around the bottom half-inch of frail crystal goblet.

"My name's Cheri," she said. "I've been watching you for months."

I stood to touch her.

Later in her room she opened her arms and for a moment looked like an expanding shadow against lamplight, dark wings spreading. I stepped nearer. Carpet muffled everything. I knew maybe I was going somewhere I shouldn't. But that seemed inconsequential now; even getting the plague seemed like a tiny thing. I was just where I'd planned on being. Stepping into the soft shadow her arms made was like stepping into a satin cloud, lightly encompassing. Blood orchid, I thought. Gossamer-exquisite, closing over a bee. Still, the bee found what it was looking for, buzzing right into the core of the bud. And when it died, it died sucking nectar.

I slid hands along her forearms until the shirt sleeves bunched. There I was, fingers trapped between flesh and silk. I kissed her lips softly, then each eyelid, on the tip of my tongue tasted salt, perfume, mascara gone bitter, hinting death, like a wine cork left to dry. I could feel her shiver. She was trying to reach me, searching for my belt. I wouldn't let her.

"Cheri, I'm going to kiss you. Or love you. Or kill you."

"Do it then, just do it."

It was liquid warm, made me think of clear water covering skin completely, reminded me of the first time I'd touched another woman's tongue with my own and the two-way shock that had gone through me then—shooting straight up into my head, obscuring every thought, then down to my belly and all parts below. But that had been so long ago. Before the war. Before the plague. Now, in this time, I could watch her eyes close while my own stayed open. I could keep my thoughts alive, despite the crazy electricity jumbling every muscle, making my breath sound faster. I could ache deep down, yet—somewhere above it all—calmly observe myself aching, and know that it did not matter.

I traced lines along the back of her neck. Reached down simply to free silk from silk once and for all. Then touched naked torso underneath. She made some sound, like a sob.

"Is it time to take your clothes off, Cheri? I think so. I think it's time."

I'd seen many breasts in my life. Hers seemed new though, a pair of something rare and beautiful: plump in a way I'd never have suspected, pink-tinged brown circling each nipple, gently puckering when I touched. I let myself get a little lost. I let hands that didn't feel like mine undo all the buttons and zippers. She ran a palm over me, between flaps of shirt. I grabbed her hand, pressed it to my mouth and licked my own sweat off.

"God," she said, "how does it taste?"

"Well, you'll find out, won't you?"

She slid down until her knees hit the carpet. Like praying, I thought. Only no words sounded. And maybe what she reached for now and took into her mouth had a different power than prayer—sacred or profane, I didn't know—but, in any case, it would not lead to salvation.

When I pulled her up she let out a louder sound and arched back onto the bed. I tugged at each silk leg. The pants peeled easily off; I didn't stop to fold them. I kissed the flesh they left behind instead, silky skin darker than my own. For a second I saw my wrist against the quivering top of her thigh, different shades of skin. The sight made me want to shut my eyes and lose myself again, but I didn't.

"Piper. Demigod. Don't kill me. Love me. Save me."

It was a whisper. Cheri twined fingers through my hair, pulled my lips up to brush belly skin, breast skin. I took nipples in my mouth again, ran my lips in circles along her neck. I could have stretched out fully on top then and kissed, long and deep. But I held myself up and apart instead, staring down at her against a background of blue satin bedcover. A gift from her father. Had it once belonged to some victim of plague? Probably. In the light her hair blended in, loose dark curls on a dark sheen. She breathed quickly, lightly. Her forehead was damp, and when she blinked the sweat gleamed.

"You're still half-dressed. No fair."

"Maybe I'm shy."

"Ah." She smiled. "We'll see." Then she toyed with zippers and leather, something opened with a clink, and for a second it felt like the rest of me would fall open too, onto satin and flesh. We moved together a little. Everything throbbed. Dancing, I thought. Slow dance. I held her hips up against me.

"Save me," she said.

"Save *that* for the minister," I said. "Your sheets, by the way—are they silk?"

They were. Dark rose-colored, fresh and smooth, the pillows goose down. I wondered if her daddy's goons had taken them, too, from the bed of another plague victim. She'd said as much. But did it matter? Did it matter to the dead? Satin cover peeled away, thick dark quilt folded underneath. I held the small of her back and watched curls spread against the rose-tinged shadow. Then eased down on top of her so our hip bones clashed, but I wouldn't go inside her, no not yet. I twined my fingers through her hair like it was some good-luck web I'd fallen into, not disaster. But gently, webs are fragile things. Her breath came against my cheek, fast, sweet. She pressed up to me, begging, and we kissed. Maybe it was the way her tongue searched under and over mine, trying to suck, then release, that made me match the sounds she was making with my own. Whispers, whimpers. That made me move in rhythm like waves on sand while Cheri strained under me, trying to catch and keep me, finally gave up and wrapped her legs around me in one wet desperate motion, nostrils flaring like something wild.

"Inside." She bit her lip raw. "Please, please. Go deep inside."

Whatever you want, I told her, you know you can have it. Here and now. Whether or not it is Sexually Righteous.

Really? she said. And sobbed.

I pulled away then, held the perfect instrument there between my own legs, found a perfect dark triangle of Cheri waiting to match it. I ran fingers through the tangled damp hair, then into a thick, open, impatient wetness that smelled faintly of the sea, and I heard her groan deep as I moved inside her against pliant wet walls, over the soft nub of something electric. Her hips swayed forward to take me in, slowly at first, then urgently. She stiffened slightly. Something like suffering went across her face.

"Ah...careful...make it last—"

I was teasingly motionless for a while, watching damp glimmer at the edges of her half-closed eyes, listening to her breathe. Then her whispers sounded raggedly, dreamily.

"I'm sick," she said. "I'm dying. I've had plague since last summer."

Something smashed the back of my neck and head. It was heavy and cold. I could hear a thud far off: my own body, half-dressed, falling.

I was standing when I woke, or rather, being held up by big hands grasping each arm. But my head dangled forward, and through the blur of swollen eyes trying to focus I could see garbage crusting each boot tip. The boots were mine, on my feet; they wobbled against the surface of expensive Persian carpeting, speckled now with tiny drops of blood. Something tickled my face. The blood was coming from me. When my neck snapped alert it ran into both ears. I could feel my collar soaked and loose—someone had taken my tie. Cheri, I thought. Remembered her curious femme fingers—trembling, unknotting. With battered lips I smiled.

"Listen. Carefully. To what I am about to tell you."

The mayor sat behind a redwood desk. The bookshelves around him were full of other people's books, dimly lit chestnut, walnut and redwood, a blur of scarlet. His goons supported me on either side, but I sensed them rather than saw. My ears rang full of blood. I could smell their sweat and mine.

"You exist because I allow you to. Because I work it out with the powers that be. Because I have pity." The mayor's voice echoed like something from the other end of a tube, his whining tenor bent, warped, the vowels elongated. He laughed. "No, not really. You live because you serve a certain purpose. Never forget that. Hamlin's full of rats and plague. Not the rats and plague you see all around you. I'm talking about the rats and plague that stream into this town like rain from all the high places, the places of money, the places of war. The rats that water your beer and dilute your medicine and sell it all back to you at black-market prices. The rats that finesse deals, barter lives for cash, make sound investments, make money from suffering and illness, make money from money and death. These rats you never see. The plague *they* spread will grip you silently, tenaciously, and you'll never even feel the terrible illness that has invaded you body and soul—as it invaded the body of my wife, and now my precious daughter—never, until the very end. But understand this, and understand it clearly: Do not underestimate the power of these rats. You live because they haven't yet bothered to kill you. Because they haven't gotten around to noticing you. But *I* notice you. And with a word, a letter from me, a memo, *they* will notice you too." He sighed. "You see, I am just middle management, really. But I shuffle the papers along."

The two goons I never saw tossed me down stone flights into the street. It was after-hours time, between four and morning. They'd taken my money, my gun, my irreplaceable pipe and, with that, my magic. Or so I thought. Then again, maybe the magic had left the second she'd turned her eyes on me. Rats ran by in the sewer, and blood dripped out of my ears for a long, long time. Until sunrise threatened and a hearse rattled by and I crawled to a corner pump for water.

It's no fun nursing a broken face. They'd stormed through my squat while I was away and wrecked everything. For many nights I shivered, half-naked, on a torn old mattress. The phone rang sometimes—once, twice, forlorn—then stopped. Whoever wanted me also did not want me or the trouble I'd bring, and I imagined her face hovering over the phone pad, fingers pressing buttons, terrorized into a grotesque ambivalence. Finally, I crawled to the bath, then staggered through the remnants of my possessions toward a splintered mirror, bruised hands fumbling as I eased into a few shredded, mottled clothes. I wrote a letter and addressed it to the mayor. Here is what it said:

*Understand that your suffering is no ticket of admission. No automatic entry badge to some illusory paradise of respect. When I come around next time you and the people you work for will pay, and receive nothing in return—except a continuation of emptiness. It is like that, emptiness: a mirror. You can see your foolish greed gazing back.*

When I limped down into the street and slipped it into a postal box, things seemed changed. There were fewer sounds than usual. The rats had multiplied so drastically that some were starving to death; they scampered around my feet feebly, blindly, their tiny ribs showing, dancing over human corpses stacked high near the trash. And the roads were deserted. Not a beggar or bum, not a hearse in sight.

I limped past one group of bodies spread out like a fan— feet toward the gutter, eyes staring open—and I recognized the preacher and his family.

*You should have loved us,* I prayed, silently. *Loved me, even me. That was your salvation. You let it pass you by.*

The Mountain was dark, windows boarded up. No notices posted. No lines at any doors. It had ceased to be that suddenly—as if a light had, just like that, been snapped off forever. Now the place was one more nailed-shut building in a long and dreary row of them on a dying city's street. Even the sign was gone.

I turned to see her watching.

Her shadowed face was puffy; someone had hit it.

"Daddy said he killed you. I came back anyway."

There was something, I thought, something I ought now to say. But I just faced her, silent.

She shrugged. It was a steadying motion, to stop herself from shivering. Fever radiated from her.

"There's a big rat in there."

"Yeah?"

"Really, really big. He's sick. He's full of plague. I think that maybe he's dying now."

I reached across the trash-strewn space of street to pull her in and hold her to me, and our bruised cheeks pressed together. Candle, I thought, light, fire. I am going to steal his fire. His future. And keep it safe somewhere as if it is a jewel or dream, somewhere protected, hidden, safe from waste and greed and plague.

"Cheri—"

"Mmmm?"

"Let's go."

It hurt to tear the boards away. Rusted nail tips scraped my flesh. Those goons had done their job, but not irrevocably.

While she watched I pulled the old door open. Something big with a whiplike tail raced past us hissing, spattering germs. She gasped. Fell into my arms. It hurt, but I lifted her up and took her in. Sealed the door behind. Inside the Mountain burned a light, from some deep part of the cellar. It dimly illuminated the busted mirrors and jukeboxes, smashed stools, tables, bar. I laid her gently down. Then stretched out next to her on the cold, cold floor, unzipped pants and reached between her legs and without even any pipe or music or magic I loved her and fucked her for hours, fucked her back to life. She came out of the death swoon from cold to hot to fever. When the fever broke with a deep, deep moan her lips and breasts were warm again, and full, and she opened her mouth and eyes.

Later we stood, dizzy. Now the power between us had shifted: I leaned against her shoulder feeling frail; she supported my tired, tired weight.

The light came from far below, from a place I'd never been. Was it war? Plague? Death? No, I thought—love! Perhaps that was just illusion—love, I mean. Yet the hope of it seemed sweet.

So we headed toward it, she and I, feeling along the walls for direction when shadows fell too strong, our shod toes inching forward. We walked knowingly somehow, though the way was strange to us.

*(1988-1995)*

# The Butterfly

*During the larval period the corpus allatum dominates. Its secretion, Juvenile hormone...controls molting as the larva progresses through several growth periods....Meanwhile, secretory cells in the brain produce brain hormone...which is actually secreted by the corpus cardiacum. Its target, the prothoracic gland, responds by secreting ecdysone, which favors the development of adult structures....The continued dominating effect...eventually influences the adult emergence.*

"Metamorphosis in a Butterfly," *Biology: The Science of Life*

There is that second where you seem to hover over the water like a haunting ghoul, in motion, yet inside the motion it feels infinitely slow. The entry headfirst, always, arms then, hand press strong, sure, outsweep, kick, both legs together, not from the knees but the hips. Hands down, elbows bent just so, and in. Sweeping. Up. Sweeping. Kick again. Then over the water neck and chest, shoulder swing, arms rotate, hip flex, in motion but slow it feels, so slow, every breath and drop an agony, a triumph, arched over the water like a fierce haunting ghoul, repetitively attacking, fearful, bursting for entry.

*Pretend you're ghosts!* coaches would yell, grimacing, baring teeth in endlessly bad cartoonish apings of something awful. *Headfirst! Rrrrrr!*

*Big kick! Baby kick!*

When we were both little-age groupers trying to win medals, my brother Jonathan and I swam butterfly.

Later, the boys adopted a different chant.

*Win!* they yelled. *Wine! And women!*

---

Over the years Jonathan's gotten used to my being gay.

Queer, I correct him sometimes, taunting, tender. Or, you know, lesbian, dyke, tribade, muff-diver.

He's even gotten used to me defiantly donning a *yarmulke* during Passover seder, a prayer shawl for Yom Kippur.

What he once said he'd never get used to, though, were all those big, sunny, friendly, fair-haired Nordic-looking girls I used to bring home for family gatherings, one after the other.

They're all-American sexy, I'd observe. That's why they make you nervous.

No, he told me. But it's like you keep picking them up in some special store that sells these perfect, pretty, good-natured WASP jock-types; you know, you finish with one, then you trade it in for the next latest model. Throwback wish fulfillment, Josie. To make up for all those swim-team types you secretly lusted after when we were growing up. Runt.

Well, runt I was. The overt invert, family disaster in more ways than one—full of desire, generally lacking talent.

Jon? He was Golden Boy, full of talent, but—and he knew that I knew—generally lacking desire.

Sure, I shot back. We both secretly lusted after those girls, Jon. But I am the one who gets them.

He scowled, blushed.

See, it's true.

The family Benvenisti? Small. Abramo can trace his lineage back to the Golden Age of southern Spain, but has few relatives. Sarah, a Holocaust survivor, has none—none, at least, since the death of Yanos. Out of mutual loneliness and loss my parents created a son and a daughter, two dark-haired, hazel-eyed, faintly olive-skinned children. Jonathan. Josefa. He. And me.

Yanos was my mother's cousin from some godforsaken little nation that, not too many decades past, had merrily sent its Jews off to death camps. We called him Uncle. A quiet, broken man, he had bad teeth and visited on weekends. He and my parents would sit companionably in the front room, not saying much. One Passover seder, when I was six and Jonathan was seven, he drank too much, took us down to the basement, undid our various buttons and zippers and poked his fingers everywhere. They were stubby fingers, I remember, the nail of the right thumb missing. Then, smiling, he dropped his pants and showed us what an Auschwitz surgeon had done.

If you tell anyone, he warned, I'll say how bad you both were.

We never did tell.

Over the next few years, mostly on holidays, I'd see him sometimes, in a breath-held sideways glance, descending into or emerging from the basement with Jonathan. Smells came to me: sweat, must, aging flesh. My brother's eyes seemed dulled and red. Later, for days afterward, he'd be unusually silent.

When I was ten and Jonathan eleven, Yanos died. My brother and I stood stiff and silent in our good dark clothes at the funeral. Afterward, on the little lawn at home, we tried to catch fireflies. Jonathan found and killed a toad. Then he stole some matches, and set the corpse on fire.

In general, Jonathan had a lot of success in the medal quest. I did not. We were just a year apart and, until adolescence, about the same size. But life happened. He continued winning the 200 butterfly; I entered a permanent slump. He was handsome, and shone. I was not, did not. Trophies, good grades, high school popularity, a macho bravado that left everyone wondering why he never dated—all these were his. Chasms spread between us.

Coach expected him to get a scholarship somewhere, somewhere good. A couple of Division I schools were definitely interested. We needed it—he did—God knows, we were not rich.

Then, about 35 yards into a very important 200 final, leading the field, he stopped dead, floated back to the starting block, got out of the pool and walked away.

He never did go back.

A week later, in his advanced chemistry class, someone set a desk on fire. They never found out who.

That afternoon I skipped practice and went home early. My brother was down in the basement, plugged into a Walkman. Some overhead bulbs had been turned on. In dull light you could see the stairs littered with butterfly wings, with their dead wingless insect bodies.

Jon, I said, what did you do?

He glared defiantly and removed the earplugs.

Nothing, he said, just got curious.

Curious about what, Jon?

What things would look like. After.


I still swim, but only recreationally.

Family visit—my first with Maddy. In the little girl's bedroom that once was mine, Maddy tells me what she thinks. A mixture of compassion for and condemnation of my family. Oh, sure, she sees their good points, but she won't forgive them for being so goddamned blind. For not asking questions, at least when the failures and troubles began. And Jonathan? Well, he doesn't like her, she can tell. Something wrong there. He's handsome and dangerous, she says, the proverbial ticking time bomb. She isn't sure she can like him, either. Although, for me, she will try.

We kiss. Talk about kisses. First times. She has been with many men, but her first kiss was with a girlfriend at the age of ten, and she knew then it was women she would love. Unless you count Yanos—should you?—I have never been with a man. She tells me what it's like, but, I confess, it seems unintriguing, perfunctory. It's her flesh, her smell, her touch that I want, that make me burn, that make me want to give her every kind of pleasure.

*Maddy, listen:* Here, in my childhood home, I will tell you more. How, for so long, love seemed willing to pass me by. High school summers spent life-guarding on the beach, watching transparent globs of jellyfish cluster mellow shorelines, car hoods lining the parking lot road twinkle like mirages in the waves of heat rising from polished fenders.

Beach umbrellas speckled the yellowish sand, colored monster mushrooms. Kids screamed and tossed plastic shovels at each other, complained loudly about the orange and green pails whose handles seemed always to twist off irreparably, sobbed that yet another beach ball had drifted out too far, rainbow stripes dotting a circle on the horizon, the circle growing smaller and smaller until it disappeared altogether. They'd capture snails, stuff them in sand-castle chambers for torture and death. Under umbrellas their mothers creamed sun-sensitive noses. I'd watch from a high white lifeguard perch, wondering how it was that these children, who had no Uncle Yanos, were so willingly curious about cruelty and murder.

Weekends the college kids were there with forbidden six-packs, rolling crotch to crotch on their towels. Weekends, all the fathers were there, dragging mats and heavy picnic baskets, tossing cigarette butts ash-down in the sand. I'd stare, above all this, from my white ladder chair, one of four along the beach. At its base, a cherry-colored surfboard. After each shift I'd take it out, paddle a half mile or so. My skin baked reddish brown and had a dusky glow. I used plenty of tanning cream, though, rarely removed my sunglasses, and was the only female on my shift—which suited me fine. One of the other guards was Jonathan. I'd watch high school girls go by that summer, watch them cluster around the base of his chair, stretching their arms to brush against the rungs, laughing in high, delicate trills that abruptly ended. The male lifeguards were youthfully muscular, casual on their thrones. It was a Catholic town, a WASP town, a factory town, and most of them were blond, pale-eyed; against the white-washed white-and-gray background, my brother glowed darkly, like some dream lover from a romance novel you'd buy in grocery stores, so all the girls watched him with a fear-tinged lust. They didn't know how damaged he was, how far away from them all. How his seemingly tantalizing remoteness was no put-on, but the very best he could manage. How their approach made him shudder inside, afraid of what anyone coming close might do, of what he might do to them. Once in a while he'd deign to take part in some conversation. Mostly, like the other boys, he flexed biceps and pectorals, pretending to ignore the girls and the dense summer heat.

Watching his anguish, I felt, for the first time, my own— my absolute difference from that pack of young women who adored him. Although I didn't yet quite comprehend its meaning or origin, I was unutterably apart from them somehow, absolutely alone. Love had passed me by. The thing they talked about in locker room showers, giggling, blushing; the thing these oblivious blonde high school girls felt following my poor crazed brother along the sand—this love was of no interest to me whatsoever. The thought of it failed to stir me. When I tried to imagine it, I was left with a feeling of emptiness.

By August, my skin had turned a deep, burnished chestnut. So had Jonathan's. I rescued two drifting beach balls before the season ended.

*Maddy, listen:* At college I tried out for the swim team but didn't make it. Had few friends. Studied something socially contributive and utterly uninteresting. Caught myself, sometimes, trying to gaze through the faces of other young women, mind's eye peeling the makeup from them to reveal fresh skin, unveiled cheekbones, untouched lips; sometimes, in this kind of reverie, I'd feel slightly embarrassed and wouldn't know why. Winter Sundays brought me face to face with unavoidable loneliness. Dull papers completed for the week, readings done, I stared through cheap dormitory windows dripping icicles and felt the ache of despair inside.

One Sunday I decided to work it off, as in the old days. I packed some necessary items and was soon trotting through white drifts on my way to the field house, once familiar territory. It was late afternoon; the pool would be nearly deserted. Wind froze my face. I blinked against the flakes blowing down from the limbs, walked as fast as possible. Only in quick motion would the internal gnawing rest. I was glad to be heading for water.

In the changing rooms of some sports-minded colleges, lockers stretch forever. They're usually gray, or lemon-colored, or the color of orange peels. On off-hour winter afternoons there is only the sound of footsteps ringing along concrete, echoing on metal. The sound of a showerhead dripping at lonely, maddening intervals, a clang of locker doors being pressed open, canvas athletic bag set on wooden bench with a gentle thud. The lighting always bleaches skin of color. Wall-length mirrors are fogged near sinks and showers; when clear, they reflect relentless pallor. Water, sweat, deodorant, the smell of hair and damp clothes, the obliterating scent of chlorine—hang unstirring in the air. When you're alone in such a place, you feel two big conflicting things: enclosed, yet revealed.

I hurried through the ritual of hanging clothes, suiting up, selecting a towel and cap. I spit into my favorite old high school goggles, then passed under a solitary shower in the row of unused stalls just outside the pool area. Good to come on a Sunday. As I'd thought, the place was nearly empty, only one other swimmer there. I watched her in appreciation. She was performing quick butterfly repeats, lots of 50s, action methodical

and rapid, the stroke nearly perfect, supremely powerful, electrifying—drops flashed silver from her fingertips with each
plunge forward, head looping down gracefully before the arms,
everything else following like the rounded, raised, descending
limbs of a dauntless, haunting ghost. Water trailed after her in
uniform ripples.

I wondered if I'd seen her before. Decided no, this was
someone from the team, maybe, but no one I knew. A thin
lifeguard lazed in his chair at the far end, reading. Even from 25
yards, I recognized the lime green textbook cover for Biology
101. But my gaze went back to the swimmer, who was resting
briefly now between repeats, goggled eyes fixed on the time clock,
fingers settled gently against her neck's pulse, counting.

I slid into sterile turquoise water. Began a slow warmup
that went nowhere. Every now and then found myself glancing
up, expectantly, watching. The swimmer had switched to longer
repeats, each interval as well-paced as a metronome.

I finished a lackluster workout that was, nevertheless, a
little relaxing. When I pressed up and out of the pool, she was
still busy a couple of lanes over—this time with perfect 50-yard
repeats again—and, you could see by the clock, she was right
on the money. This was immediately humbling but somehow
pleasing, and I retreated to the showers, soon back to the long,
deserted locker room, dripping clean and naked onto a towel
spread bench-wide, shaking out my lycra cap, drying goggle
lenses, sorting through a bag for skin cream. The mirror steamed
slightly, reflected some blurred image back. I avoided looking
that way. Mirrors bothered me. Still, whenever I did look, sideways as if stealing, I realized how much I wanted her to appear
from the shower entrance behind: that swimmer with the electrifying butterfly, looming suddenly into life on land. The mirror fogged. I felt my heart pound with a different, brutal thud.
Outlines of a suited body had indeed appeared, as hoped for, plain
white towel thrown over one careless, smooth broad shoulder.

I turned. She was in a dark suit. She still wore cap and goggles and, approaching the mirror, looked like some strange, blank, faintly cruel creature from space—head smoothed to bright round baldness, eyes obscured. She looked strong and bold, almost strutting as she moved with chest wide and breasts proud, nipples erect, pointing forward. I turned back clumsily to my skin cream. Blushing. Felt water drip from cheeks to towel. Stole one last blurred glimpse of myself and the woman, strange swimmers in a mirror. Then I became aware of a subtle burning in the corner of one eye. A tear slid silently out to join the rest of what speckled my face. It hit me full force at that moment: I was alone, and filled with desire.

This seemed, suddenly, to be the source of all dark things: the hollow ache that kept me up at night; the pain of family, of childhood. Without knowing why, I raised my head again to the mirror, gazed fully at it—not at myself, but at the anonymous swimmer who stood there staring coolly at both our fogged images. Silly me. I couldn't have known how much it showed on my face: desire. That desperate, pained yearning for love, however it might come. The look must have left my face open and raw for the first time in years. And then, because of this or in spite of it, and for just one racing second, I saw something else bloom on it: a certain torn beauty that was no longer adolescent, that some woman, somewhere, might love.

All this was news to me. First times take us by surprise. So I couldn't have known, couldn't have seen how clearly it was witnessed.

The other woman turned slowly. There was something regal in the motion, haughty, almost calculated. She approached with calm, slow steps that were graceful on the damp floor tiles. Entirely female and familiar, and at the same time unknowable, a creature from the water with eyes obscured, head rounded smoothly by a cap that thousands wore. She was well-formed but unknown, completely unidentifiable as anything but a woman and a swimmer. Close up, her features seemed blander still, with that unyielding alien quality. Desire and cruelty hovered in the damp air, hovered over my own broad shoulders, my upturned face.

Then it melted.

She leaned down in one smooth motion and her transformation was complete: from brutal water creature to angel of mercy. Dripping hands planted firmly on my shoulders, she kissed me full on the mouth. And a thrill rippled through—the otherness of the touch, sudden invasion of an unknown tongue against my own—it rippled up and down my neck and along my spine in a continuous wave, caused my ears to burn, forced my nipples instantly erect, thighs to shiver strangely as they never had before.

Had I thought about it logically, maybe I would have been a little appalled. That all the handsome, sometimes friendly boys and men I had seen in my life had failed to arouse me, while this anonymous woman, with whom I had no discernible connection, could move me to the edge of some unidentified high and glorious cliff by a mere touch of wet lips and tongue.

But I thought of nothing then. There was only sensation, and it washed through me quickly. Some locker room door groaned open down an aisle. The kiss ended abruptly. Then my angel of mercy retreated, hovering remotely away along the length of mirror. She turned without a single look back, vanished among the rows of lockers.

I walked in the snow that night. Slightly demented. That love would show its face to me this way—I had trouble absorbing it. It had been disguised, really, by water apparatus, cut short by the creak of door hinges. Entirely outside all the rule books and regulations, a love of which no age-groupers' coach would have approved.

I am crying a little. Maddy licks the tears.

I just got all wet, listening, she says. Get on top of me, baby.

Here, in my childhood room, the bed creaks up and down.

We are all getting older. Jonathan's thirty-three now. And, he says, beginning to understand why Mom and Dad always carried on so much about the importance of family. Nowadays, he says, he feels that way too. Wants to reconnect—with them, with me. He tells me that, in therapy, he has learned how love is good. He has become less dangerous, he thinks, to himself, to others.

We will see.

He's itching for accolades, I can tell. About to finish his residency at a good hospital. Engaged to marry—a woman! Shoshana, who is visiting relatives in Tel Aviv now, but would otherwise be here, with us all, for the weekend.

I have a name for his bride-to-be: GIT—the Gorgeous Israeli Tease.

She seems to make him happy. Or, at any rate, proud.

Me? I finally decided what I wanted to do, and passed the EMT training course. Blood doesn't bother me. Neither does pain. They have rotated me to the day shift.

Also, I have love now. I have Maddy.

And I have this dream: Maybe my brother and I are approaching neutral ground again. Closeness, even. Without fear. Envy. Pity. Yanos. The butterfly.

In early middle age, maybe, we'll be friends.

In between, though—somehow, in a way neither of us understands—there is Maddy.

One of your *shiksa* types again, he says.

It isn't really true, at least not like before. All those other women I showed off to prove some point. That one way or another I could fuck them, whereas maybe he could not. But this woman I love.

We are married.

My wife? Yes, actually. Plump filling in the contours of a

sturdy, once-slender body, her short-bobbed fair hair starting to streak with gray. She has a terrific face marred here and there by old acne scars. Wears makeup and loose-fitting flowery dresses. Everything set off by big, bright, cool evaluative eyes that take no hostages.

And Maddy, too, is here for the weekend.

You and Maddy are really going to like each other, I promise.

Mom's busy in the kitchen, Dad rustling around the front yard. I stash our overnight bags. Quietly, in a big chair in my old bedroom, Maddy sits.

With his whiskey sour half finished, Jonathan tries to break the ice. I rummage inanely through hangers in an empty closet, letting this first thing that is happening between them resonate faintly in the background.

"Hiya, Maddy."

"Hi."

"Can I get you anything?"

"No, thanks."

"Well, I'm glad to finally meet you. My sister says we'll like each other. Not that it matters—I mean, as long as *you* like *her.*"

She leans forward, eyes full of a strange humor he cannot quite recognize. "I love your sister, Jonathan."

"Good. Well—that's good."

"What about you?"

"Me?"

"Do you love somebody?"

"As a matter of fact, I do."

"Good," she says. "Lucky for your patients."

Uh-oh.

The bed is right there; he sits, probably warily. "My patients?"

"Sure. You're going to be a surgeon, right?"

"Am," he says. It comes out bitterly, and I wonder why. "I already am a surgeon."

"Oh, okay. Say you had to go under the knife. You wouldn't want somebody fiddling around inside you, would you, who didn't know the first thing about love?"

"I guess not."

My brother suspects the bitch is patronizing him, but can't really tell.

My Maddy—yes, she is a bitch. One of the reasons I fell for her. Flipside of all that softness that can pull you right down on top and inside it so that you never want to leave. It's her armor—the bitchiness, I mean—the femme ferocity a bullet-proof vest that covers her, and me.

I do worry for his patients.

Maddy smiles then, so gently. I can tell without looking. It's an engaging smile, female soft, the teeth imperfect but white.

She helps my mother prepare dinner. Sarah protests, but it's for show. Despite herself, she likes this—girlfriend? lover?— this *wife* of mine, Maddy's easy female chatter, the expert way she slices vegetables gently, how she cores the iceberg lettuce with one deft whack on the side of the sink, washes everything thoroughly, cleans up after. The details of survival—sleep, sustenance, sanitation—are important to Sarah, more important than anything else. Not just women's work, but the life and breath of the world; and, after all, she ought to know. I hear them talking through walls, around corners, yakking away. My mother senses that, in some way, Maddy is also a survivor. They share much more than they'll ever consciously know. Both have done just what they had to do, at times, to get by. In retrospect, some of the things they had to do were rather unpleasant; one might even say immoral.

But who sets standards of morality these days? God? The same God who watches holocausts and all manner of suffering with a cool, indifferent eye? Who watched our Uncle Yanos in the basement?

I'm not impressed.

Later, we dine. Roast beef. An intentional or unintentional slight—I've been a vegetarian for years. On the other hand, a way of honoring Maddy. I watch her, and Jonathan, over a mountain of string beans. Catch Maddy examining his handsome, sullen face. But my features are less smooth than his, even though I'm younger, bitten by harsh dyke things and by sorrow here, tangible and intangible loss you'd think would show on him too by now, craggy and sharp where Jonathan's are rounded. I notice him glancing back; and, I notice, so does Maddy. He's looking a little smug, my brother. Adding the pieces of her up. Surmising, correctly, that the eye shadow and foundation probably hide a few of the blocks she's been around.

This sneaky evaluation is something my Maddy has come to expect from men. Frankly, she says, she finds it a bore. Granted, the truth probably wouldn't make appropriate dinner conversation, but were my brother to openly ask, Maddy would have no problem telling him about the years she spent jerking guys off in massage parlors to make a living. And that, sure, she does more middle-class things nowadays to pay rent—clerical, secretarial, whatever. But she's never been the type of girl to lie much, or to suffer undue shame about the past. Women do what they have to do to get by at the time. No more, no less.

Jonathan has puckered lines of worry across his forehead. Maddy, who sees everything, has already seen this. I know what she's dying to tell him: Honey, what you need most in your life is a good blow job. Trust me. And, by the way, that gorgeous, full-lipped, selfish-eyed girl I've seen in photographs, the one you're about to marry, will probably never give you one.

If only that were the answer.

Thankfully, it's his problem. Not, bless Maddy, his sister's.

My mother and I put food away, clean dishes. Maddy's making friends with Dad, trying to charm him, and every once in a while, through the splash of green cleansing bubbles and running water, I can hear her laugh echo faintly from the den. Dutifully stacking things in the drainer while my mother washes and rinses, I'm thankful for this older woman's quiet dignity. For years, now, she has accepted my sexual destiny with seeming serenity, certainly without comment. Maybe it's due to a lack of willingness to confront painful truths.

On the other hand, there are some truths better left alone. They tend to caper around more freely, these truths, when they are not shoved right into your face. Sarah's difficult life will not be made more complete, by any stretch of the imagination, if I bothered to tell her that, for the last decade or so, her only daughter has been buckling leather harnesses around her hips, attaching silicon rubber dildos of various sizes thereto, and using this equipage to enthusiastically fuck other woman as often as possible.

Had Jonathan turned out gay, I think, certain truths could not have been so successfully avoided.

What then?

Would my mother's life have been enhanced by knowing exactly what her sole surviving relative did? Would she understand that it filled her children's lives with sorrow? Dimmed her only son's bright promise? But that it did not, did not, did not make me queer? That loving women have healed me, being queer has been my salvation? That my goddess, my angel, was a woman swimming butterfly? So that what I am today, what Maddy and I have together, makes up the beautiful and triumphant part of things, not the tragic?

That Jonathan is still unhealed? And dangerous?

All talk of this seems, somehow, easy to escape. A man tried to destroy me, but a butterfly saved me. She did not save my brother. This would be difficult to prove. He's done nothing but kill a toad, set a fire, quit a race, gone through med school. A bright and golden boy. Who once I knew. Who once I loved.

Should I go to the police? Tell them, Look here, I have a feeling that my brother, upstanding citizen, outstandingly handsome heterosexual male specimen, up-and-coming doctor, is insane? That he may do something terrible someday?

Should I tell Shoshana?

No one would believe me.

In the end, maybe there is little we can do about anything. We're a private species with plenty of secrets. If humans were meant to live in controlled fishbowl environments, we'd all have been born guppies. And I don't like anyone, even Sarah, staring at pieces of my life that, after all, I cannot really change. Why should he?

My mother has a deep intuitive understanding of certain things: basically, some qualities are immutable. People can be bad sometimes, or good. Full of ignorance and terror, or full of curiosity.

Curiosity itself can be healthy or psychotic. Your average doctor is curious about prolonging life; your average Nazi doctor about prolonging death.

She told me once that each child begins life full of energy and fear. At life's end, she said, we are less afraid, but also much more tired. So that being a death camp survivor, in the final analysis, could not make you better or worse than anyone else. Just a good deal more exhausted.

And I love her for this, though she doesn't know it: things like personality, psychological trauma, sexuality or lack thereof are, to her, a drop in the bucket of life. It's the bucket itself—the living, breathing life—that she knows is important. In her own damaged European way, Sarah is totally cool. Always sees the big picture.

Although the details, like Yanos, do tend to elude her.

We're finished washing and stacking and drying. The door to the den's closed. Jonathan is in there, Maddy says, with my father, having some kind of a man-to-man. We women share

tea, Maddy and my mother hunched close in a weird conspira-
torial silence at the kitchen table. I am near the door in my
tilted-back chair, ankle over a knee, boylike.

What are they doing in there for so long, father and son?
My dad, I think, is comfortable in his armchair. Schnapps swirl-
ing in a shot glass. He'll drink it slowly, the way he did every
night of our childhood, swishing each meager mouthful up
against the insides of his teeth with a liquid clicking sound, as if
it's his last taste of schnapps on earth. A late-night rerun of the
*McNeil-Lehrer News Hour* or something will disturb the den's
low-lit serenity—some news broadcast, always a news broadcast, for he likes to know, to know, to know. Even though, as
usual, mostly terrible things have occurred during the last twenty-
four hours; even though, as usual, he can do nothing about any
of it. Abramo muttering at the screen, shaking his head. The
conversation will go something like this:

"Bastards. Kill them all."

"Who, Dad?"

"Better yet, let them kill each other. Bunch of Nazi scum.
How does it feel, scum? How does it feel, now that you don't
have the Jews to kick around any more?"

Jonathan will know without looking: Bosnia. When he
settles into the sofa, though, Dad turns it off. Silently wishing
that he does not have to go through all this fuss, that Jonathan
and Shoshana would just elope. But he raises his glass in one
thick, steady, working man's liver-spotted hand. "Cheers."

"Cheers."

"Your mother wants me to talk to you about the wedding."

Gifts. Money. Arrangements. Invitations and exclusions. I
still know my brother—at least, a little. Alarm will prick his
spine, and everything he's been meaning to say—*Look, Dad, I
thought I'd tell you first, Shoshana and I have decided to elope.
And oh, by the way, remember Uncle Yanos? Well, he raped both
your kids in the basement one night. I think it made me crazy—*

will desert him in a kind of panic. In his mind he'll see himself diminished, a small, frail boy, racing futilely around a windy lawn to retrieve the shredded pieces of a firefly, a toad, a childhood, of some important document.

On my childhood bed, Maddy and I are getting there.

When my brother walks along the hall, past the basement door, past the mostly closed door meant to hide us well, he stops for a second to watch. It's not something he was meant to see, for sure. But there he is anyway, curious; and here we are—never mind that the bed's made and our clothes are on—practically in flagrante delicto. Maddy on her back, face turned passionately against a pillow, legs spread to straddle me as I rock, gently, smiling, between them. Every once in a while her lips part, a soundless moan. Her eyes are closed. When they flick open to see the shadow he makes in the partly open crack of doorway, her hand, which has been spread across my back, flexes warning, and the motion we're making together stops.

Jonathan flees. Down the hall to his own room with a face burnt red. Probably half aroused, half nauseated, I think. And wishes like hell he hadn't seen us—the close, almost delicate, generous motion of two women's bodies pressing into one another, prelude to something unspeakably exquisite. What will he do? Turn on a lamp, grab the thumb-worn copy of *Gray's Anatomy* from a bedside table, searching out ligaments, tendons, cartilage to cut.

But it's too late. Flushed, we're standing; Maddy's chasing him. I follow her out into the hallway, listening, watching, halfway between my childhood bedroom and his, right in front of the shut-tight basement door, a tired and violent no-man's land, stuffy with memory.

She leans into his room.

Under makeup, Maddy blushes. The steely eyes are furious.

"What are you, some kind of creep?"

"Me?"

"You. I saw you looking."

"Why don't you two just close the door, Maddy?"

She pouts. And he must wonder, intrigued by the utter female prettiness of it, if she does that to get her way with me sometimes too, and if so, does it work?

Yes, Jon. And—yes.

When she speaks, though, any vestige of childishness has vanished. I listen, amused, desperate. "Okay, Jonathan. You and I are in serious trouble already, I can tell. Are we going to work it out or not?"

"Work what out, Maddy?"

"You. Me. Our relationship."

I can imagine him, putting his hands up half-mast, as if staring down the barrel of a gun that hasn't been cocked yet. "Whoa there, whoa! Your relationship is with my sister, doll!"

"Yes, right. And therefore with you. Has it occurred to you, at all, that we're in-laws?"

"In-laws?"

"Sure, you know, like that wife of yours will be whenever you do all the brouhaha. Well, Josie and I are married, too."

"What? You mean, ceremonially?"

"Yes, sure, and in our hearts." Her left hand flashes, extravagantly. There it is, second to last finger, what I gave her, band of gold.

"Three weeks ago, Jonathan. Central Park. Some friends read our vows. Then we went down to City Hall and registered. You know, as partners."

"You can do that?"

"Oh God, honey, get a life!"

"How do you like that. She never even told me."

"She almost called. Then she cried. She loves you, Jonathan— you should hear how she talks about you sometimes. It's as if, growing up, you were everything. You anchored her to the world and you didn't even know it. Personally, so far, I think you're a sick, selfish, narcissistic fart. But if she loves you, I have to consider the fact that maybe you're worth loving. So you and I have this choice now. Are we going to break the ice? Don't we have to? Because one thing I won't let anyone, anyone in the world do, is hurt her. Not you, not me, not anybody! I'd scratch your eyes out, mister, if I thought you'd even try."

I imagine him, staring at her with that look he wears instead of defeat, a mixture of hate and admiration. For a moment, there's silence, a silence in which I know, somehow, what he will not say: That, like me, he just wants to be home again sometimes, safe and sound. That there is no home for us anywhere, anymore, and maybe never was, unless it is inside ourselves.

When he speaks, the words move toward me down the hallway, echoing, vile, off the cold locked dust of the basement door.

"Christ, Maddy. Next time you want to break the ice, remind me to bring my blowtorch." He grins. "Or my scalpel."

I retreat for the night. Before all this there was the hot wet feel of sex about to happen. Now, given the opportunity, I would rather shoot thorazine. But Maddy insists. Partly out of desire, I think, mostly out of stubbornness and pride—she's not about to let my family desexualize us, she says, not now or ever, not if she has anything to do with it. Which, of course, she does.

I do what I can in the way of submission, knowing that tonight it will soothe her ego: letting her touch me a little, but not inside. She accepts that. Whispering in my ear never mind but to fuck her, fuck her, please.

Well, I can always do that.

I wonder if Jonathan hears us through the walls, if he even listens. If it arouses him, or sickens him; makes him think of Shoshana, or old races, or of butterflies. If he can love his woman, too, and please her, and make her moan; and if sometimes, as

Maddy has taught me, she has taught him the sweet power of surrender.

Later, Maddy sleeps. I stay awake. Listening for what I think might happen, rustlings, and footsteps.

I am Jonathan's sister, for sure. Almost a twin in some ways. Since the thing with Yanos, neither of us has slept well. Tonight, insomniac or exhilarated, full of psychotic or sane energy or both, we cannot possibly sleep. I listen through walls. Hear my brother tossing. Throwing off blankets and throwing on an undershirt, pulling denim cutoffs over his boxers. In my room I do the same. Sitting then standing, carefully, while this lover sleeps. Lacing up smelly old running shoes with holes in the toes. I follow after him the way I've done all my life, runt trailing bro, like a cub following papa bear's scent down the hall, through flimsy locks and rusted screen doors, until both of us, runt and bro, queer and straight, disappointment and triumph, are out in the night. But only he believes he's alone. Crossing wet grass, following pockets of light spread by streetlamps.

Jonathan moves quickly across lawns, skirts hedges, wiggles through rusted-out holes in aluminum fences, follows old paths into narrow clusters of spruce and maple. He does it by instinct, and I follow—or is it something more deeply ingrained than conscious memory? How many times did we do this as kids? Shortcuts. Somersaulting lightly over one barrier or another to trespass. The one place where, yes, both of us were forbidden.

Back then, when it was a mostly WASP and Catholic town of sparse privilege and unspoken genteel prejudice, the place we are heading for was restricted. Now, they've let in some Jews, and an Asian or two.

Still, even in the old days, nothing ever kept us out at night. A few stone walls. Bridged barricades. Past fading signs saying MEMBERS ONLY, across the falsely rolling greens and sands of a man-made golf course. Parking lot. Club dining room. Pool house. Over a waist-high freshly white-painted barrier. My brother vaults and I watch. He lands right next to the lifeguard's chair, and the smell hits him, hits me: damp northeastern breeze of late summer, grass, chlorine, concrete. It stretches off into the dark, touched only by a leaf here, a bug there—fifty meters of water, this specially preserved enclave into which, as kids, equally excluded, we trespassed with terror and glee.

Jonathan pulls off shirt and shoes. When he unzips the cutoffs they fall, loosely, simply, and he steps out of them clad only in boxers and hint of a beer gut. The floating lanes have been taken out and coiled heavily on land, many hours ago. The rectangular expanse of water is all his now, he thinks, undivided sideways, lengthwise. All his. And mine. He sticks in a toe.

"Come on, Jon. Go for it."

My voice should have startled him into turning around; instead, he dives. Luckily, into the deep end. There is that almost unfelt rush of the air. Up, over, down. Kick back with the legs. Head aiming between the shoulders now, a little lower, deep. I vault the waist-high fence. Settle cross-legged by the side of the pool, watching this man, my brother, who once I loved, who once I knew, splash like a boy in the water. He shuts his eyes and I feel it with him, gushing past his ears, up his nose, torturous, chilling, wet. How, in that first moment of contact with the substance, his life rolls behind both eyelids like a stunningly fast videotape: Mom Dad Josie, Shoshana. A dog we had once, long ago. Crushing bright leaves in the autumn. Does he think of trophies won? Youth passed? The 200 fly? Uncle Yanos? Childhood lost? Does he even remember? Now he's bobbing up, opening his eyes—chlorine stings them, I know—shocked to be breathing. Racing dive. Not bad, he chuckles, and we both feel it—his surprise easing away. Not bad, no, not too bad, for a weird doctor with a beer gut.

"Right, Jon. Just a touch too deep."

"Shut up!"

"Hmmmph." I sit motionless at the side of the pool. If there were any lights, he'd see me smile.

He treads shakily, doesn't sink, then relaxes and the movements get easy. All there, after all, in the muscles. When your mind forgets, the body remembers. Wind rushes through his lips, through mine.

"So you got married, huh?"

I nod. See him catch it, barely visible, a motion like a sound.

"And you didn't even tell me—"

"Well, Jon. It was kind of private."

"Bullshit."

"Okay, okay. I just got afraid. I mean, afraid, okay? But also tired."

"Tired?"

"Sometimes. Yeah. Of explaining myself. Do it enough, it hurts, you know. And it does get boring."

He dips his face in and blinks, arms moving slowly, effortlessly, as if he is in a perfect time warp, young again, and strong. Used to the water now aren't you, my brother, and it no longer feels foreign, just faintly refreshing, summer warm, life itself. Like something you were born to.

"Shit, Josie. That—lady of yours. She's quite a character."

"Maddy makes me happy."

"Well, she loves you."

"Oh," I say, softly, "I know."

"You're lucky. Tell me something, do you ever think about it?"

"Love?"

"No. Yanos."

I shake my head. Then sigh. "Oh, all the time. Mostly with murderous intent. But the thing is, Jon, that motherfucker was so damaged himself. One holocaust that never stopped, right? It went right on going, came right into our lives."

"College, one year."

"Yeah?"

"I got charged with shoplifting. Surgical supplies, books, psychiatric diagnostic manuals—I wanted to find out some name for what I was. That's where you queers are lucky, ducky. You've got a name. And it's not even in the DSM these days."

"Well, it isn't an illness, schmuck. Other things are."

Warm drops fall from his lips when he laughs. "God, Josie, I stole so much! Anyway, they sentenced me to ten hours of community service and a month of counseling. The month turned into years. It's under control now, too."

"Maybe you shouldn't get married, Jon."

"I'd never hurt Shoshana."

I think: Run, Shoshana, run.

Alone in the water, my brother sobs. He speaks freely, like a kid, telling me he's remembering a bunch of things—winter, his senior year of high school. Short course. Indoor. That particular meet, an important one. Yes. Division I coaches watching. His race. Two-hundred fly. One and a half laps and he thought of Yanos, pulled up dead in the water, mid-lane, went vertical and treaded and watched seven other boys splash ahead into the future. Then surfed slowly to the wall, hauled himself out, and quit, just walked away. Somewhere, off in the background, he heard me yelling—for him, not at him—heard my wounded cries. As he walked past the bleachers, head down, eyes trained on the wet tiled floor, he was careful to glance up once at me—in rage, in a kind of unspeakable triumph, eyes blazing something horrible. Look, they said, Hitler won.

What glory it would have been, he knew now, just to finish a thing out. How he had learned, finally, to respect and admire me. Not because of my losses, really, but the way I had handled them. How it had buried itself inside him since. That fear, that terror, the suspicion that, whatever the upcoming crisis, he would not have it in him. How it had formed and deformed his life.

I know that some of this is bullshit. But, out of respect for the way he is trying to get close to me again, I keep my mouth shut.

"You remember?"

"Sure, Jon."

"Lap and a half. Christ. I have never forgiven myself. Not in all these years. You still swim sometimes, huh?"

He waits in the dark now—for something. I search inside to give it. Find it missing. Know that he is lost, and the hour too late; I cannot save him. Queer, straight, both dealt the same damage. One of us survived. Who would have thought, looking back, that I'd be the one.

"Josie?"

"What, love?"

"Before I hurt her, I'll kill myself."

Is it my imagination, or does something inside him, some last vestige of brilliance and love, surge up, break apart? It's shining between us now, a little ball of fire, anger, compassion. Final shreds of sanity he has used to fight his pain. It will burn itself out quickly, in the night. Before it does, though, he will use it, ride it. Offer it to me as a gift. I see this all quite clearly. Watch him see it, too. Maddy's right: he's the ticking bomb, waiting to explode. At the same time, he knows what I know. But the last great wish is love.

"Win!" he sobs. Then, "Wine! And women!"

My doomed brother ducks under and surfaces, breathing air so hot it must feel like fire on his tongue. Then he turns away from me as I sit cross-legged there in the damp and dark, faces the night-obscured far-off end. Maybe, I think, he can feel me grin. Two hundred long ones. In that second we are part of the same flesh and blood again. And both of us know, too, just what it is he'll do. Now, right here—and later.

"I love you, Jon."

But he's silent. Beyond all that, and waiting for permission.
I cry inside. I let him go.
"Okay, sweetheart. Swim."
Butterfly.
He takes the last breath of the world. Dives under with all
his dangerous male might, dolphins perfectly, surfaces, feet to-
gether, big kick baby kick, arms and shoulders spanning the dark
wet like a terrible vast-winged bird.

*(1979-1993)*

# The Last Birthday of Vita Sackville-West

*for my mother*

As she grew older, the faces of children seemed to take on a strange new quality.

It wasn't anything she'd have bothered to explain to her own grown children now, on the day of her final birthday. It probably would have hurt their feelings, and she would not have meant it to. But, it was true, with advancing years—especially when traveling, gazing into the smeared, food-hungry, love-hungry little foreign faces looking up—she had gotten the eerie feeling that *these* were her children, too; that, in fact, she could have cared for them just as much as she had her very own. Sometimes, in jungles and on deserts and in miserable garbage-soaked city streets, their small, sunburnt heads had seemed surrounded by a soft, almost electric glow.

Here, at home, a private loving family urged her to blow out candles and open gifts.

There were things she'd have liked to tell them. That her passion for them was eternal, even though softened with time. That she'd have unhesitatingly laid down her life for each one of them, but that they had not made up all of her life, in the end. There were also others who had molded and twisted and adored and betrayed her. She entertained certain special old romantic notions, dreams, memories of kisses and of alien, forbidden tears that had never died. Other wishes. Other loves.

The mind plays endlessly. It creates daydream lands of infinite possibility.

Maybe, right now—right now! in some parallel universe— she was nobody's mother or wife but someone wealthy, cruel, selfish, extravagant, and solitary instead. In yet another universe—now, right now—she was young and male, astride a high-tailed steed. Or yet again, a space traveler staring breathlessly, weightlessly out at the unshielded brilliance of stars.

These worlds went on and on.

She'd have told them that along with uncountable words and deeds, her life had been filled with silences. Moments she had let pass without comment, later wishing for them back—or glad they had gone. Times when her own emotions had been unspeakable. Her own existence unbearable. When she had not loved herself, or life, and had simply pushed on anyway. When she had felt her own passion and desire irrevocably lost, dissipated like the steam from cooking pots. Then there had been duty, responsibility; there had been the roles you assumed in each and every life, those fateful and eventually doomed external appearances the price you paid for human existence. But the masks and costumes you willingly or unwillingly took on, that sometimes you experienced as revolting burdens, were also, sometimes, the only things that would save you. So that, repeatedly, you stood kneeling in the garden dirt, plucked thistles from your knees, watched tears dissolve into earth. Or stuffed tissue up your nose and unlocked the bathroom door. Accepted your lot. Went back out to change a diaper. To be a mother or a wife. To wear the flesh and the cloth. Again to join the party.

The man she had married many decades ago was her good friend now. Her children, all grown, were also friends. Perhaps, looking and waiting, they faintly sensed these thoughts.

I do not care if you marry, she wanted to tell them. Or have children of your own, or accumulate material wealth, or attain some kind of power. None of these things are important. Achieve them if you want. Do not achieve them for me. Meaning lies in a purpose fulfilled. Our human purpose is not, must never be, mere contemplation—for how can one transcend what one has never experienced?—but rather, active love. In all of its sweat and striving, clumsy effort, physical odor, its muddled mess and damage.

And for her now, reflection.

Fireplace. Friends. Birthday cake.

Faces that surrounded her. She could feel the glow.

It is the same soft electric glow of children's faces, you know, when you see them in the jungle or in deserts or on starving city streets, that sometimes renders these objects of love peculiarly and utterly interchangeable, and it is in them but also in you, in what happens in the meeting of the *I* and the *you,* that one finds it. It is why we belong to each other in a compassionate but oddly impersonal way in the end: this web of light that binds us.

Fire flared. Her family was waiting, grown up but laughing and crying quietly now, even childishly.

She smiled back—for them. Then blew out all the candles.

*(1993)*

# Love and Death, & Other Disasters

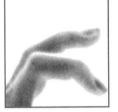

*Disease, health! Spirit, nature! Are those contradictions? I ask, are they problems? No...the recklessness of death is in life, it would not be life without it.... Death is a great power. One takes off one's hat before him, and goes weavingly on tiptoe...Reason stands simple before him, for reason is only virtue, while death is release, immensity, abandon, desire. Desire, says my dream. Lust, not love. Death and love—no, I cannot make a poem of them, they don't go together. Love stands opposed to death. It is love, not reason, that is stronger than death....And with this—I awake.*

Thomas Mann, *The Magic Mountain*

Michael stumbled into bed with them early morning, the way he did most Sundays. Callie had been used to it for years. The Oedipal complex didn't require a *male* father and *female* mother, she knew—just a couple of adults sharing intimacy would do. Kids had extraordinary radar for it. One wet unguarded kiss, one groan of passion through a bedroom door, and they'd be there like white on rice.

This time, though, she and Pat hadn't even got around to it. They hadn't, in fact, for weeks, though both had at times been willing. A waste of Pat, Callie knew. Pat who was strong and soft-butch handsome in her way, who could be smart and tender. But something in them, between them, had lately conjured uncertainty. Maybe all the stuff with Lu, Callie'd speculated in therapy. No shit, her shrink replied.

Groggy-eyed now, the kid disturbed nothing, just tumbled over a mess of sheets in the dark and wedged himself firmly between the fully-clad two of them.

"Callie."

"What, Mike?"

"Mom Lu's dying."

"I know she's dying, honey."

"No, no, I had a dream." He was half conscious but insistent, his breath a pastiche of sleep, toothpaste, spit. "She's dying *now*."

Then he slept while something inside Callie burned stark awake, and she stayed that way until the digital clock blinked 6:00 A.M. in green, a lightening gray sky began to shimmer through blinds, and the phone drilled once, twice, stopped—a signal. When ringing resumed she was up and at it, not even bothering to say hello, knowing that, with the weird synchronicity that evolves among those holding long, exhausting vigils, Françoise would understand it was she who'd answered, Callie, and simply begin talking. And, of course, she did. The tones were hushed, husky, accented. Once Callie'd loathed them. Now, though, they were just inescapably familiar: Françoise's voice and the terrifying news it conveyed merely what she'd learned to hear, listen to, stop hating over time.

Cabbing to the hospice she was, as usual, plenty hurt and scared. She took it out on Freud this time. Repeating the personal mantra hotly, silently: Eros and Thanatos, Eros and Thanatos, Eros, Eros, well fuck *you,* buddy! Fuck you and your fucking *Eros!* When what I need is agape. When what I need is love. When what I *really* need is an extra thirty bucks for cab fare today.

When what *she* needs is time.

Which was it in the proverbial nutshell, anyway. The whole trouble with Lu, both BC and AC—before and after cancer—there was never enough time. Not for her. Or for anyone else. On fouled winter sleet the taxi veered alarmingly close to a bike messenger who turned once, giving them the finger, then sped through a red light. Torn vinyl pricked her thighs. Exhaust clouding out like breath around all the closed windows made her think of that hazy half-dream time after sex and before blessed sleep—shit, she was tired—and she shut her eyes longingly.

Once, she and Lu had had a glimpse of the leisurely passionate serenity they'd always promised each other but had never really delivered—years ago in Provincetown, early autumn. A fading hint of summer on the wind, cloudless sky, seagulls circling briny morsels near the shoreline. They'd found their deserted, forbidden spot, spread one old blanket underneath and another half over, spent the entire day fucking in the dunes. At Lu's instigation and insistence. Callie had been surprised. Because, of course, she was usually the one wanting, Lu the one withholding. Yes, what her shrink called that tired old good cop/bad cop crap had got set in stone early on between them. This time, though, was different. And they'd both sensed it in a single electric touch of lips and tongues. The touch diffused, spread, widened in a caress that amazed in its softness and strength, and then the slow thoughtless peeling off of clothes, pressing together of more and more skin, until everything felt like one big aching cunt and they were all over each other in a sweet, sweet urgency. It wasn't finished after the first time but happened again. And again. The blankets shifted. Sand got in their hair. And something that had always been there blocking their way to one another, a thing the unmovable stone difference had always seemed writ large on, fell away. They looked at each other fearlessly, caressed and begged and fucked deep, deep inside. Once that afternoon, Callie on her back—which, she'd

freely admit, was her favorite place to be when Lu was around—
she'd looked up delirious, raw-eyed, to see her lover's face stripped
and naked, staring down. Big, charismatic Lu who attracted
everyone but had somehow chosen her. Athlete's body, scholar's
mind. Lu worked hard at both. All that long, well-muscled flesh
trapped hers beneath, the thick, fatless thighs and broad, broad
shoulders—a body that almost always made Callie feel impov-
erished by comparison, self-conscious and flabby. But not today.
The words had spilled out of her then, sans thought or reason,
crazy, whispered.

"God, Lu. Give me a baby."

"Yes," Lu breathed, "okay," and put her whole hand inside.

Later, showered and dressed, after a cafe dinner, strolling
the shadowy, empty town lanes in chillier twilight, they'd dis-
cussed logistics. Arthur's sperm, Callie decided. He was a mutual friend and had already volunteered, not to mention the
lucky fact that his horror of anal penetration, of oral sex, of
sharing bodily fluids—or, for that matter, of ever engaging in
any sort of intimacy at all—had left him fat, alone, anxious to
baby-sit, and HIV-free. Near Commercial Street, the first fallen
leaves brushed their shoes. They paused short of a pool of
lamplight and hugged. She could feel her legs still wobbly from
the day's emotion and orgasm. They shivered against Lu's stronger, longer ones. Feeling it too, Lu smiled teasingly.

"Did the earth shake, little rabbit?"

"Oh shut up, Lu," she purred, but they were already moving apart.

Michael's birth, his first years, had brought them together
again in that fierce, timeless cocoon of borderless protective love,
had seemed to close all the gaps between them. For a while.

Time betrayed her again. The cab stopped at the right place
much too soon. And the driver turned, unexpected kindness in
his eyes.

"Visiting someone?"

"Yes."

"Uh-huh. Well, good luck."

"Thank you," she said, "thanks a lot." Truly grateful.
Handing over the money, though, she noticed how gingerly he took it, pinching the edge of the wad so that their fingers would not clumsily meet. The kindness in his eyes was fear, she saw; her own brief gratitude, anger.

"It's not contagious, pal."

"What's that?"

"Cancer. I mean, as far as we know. Although some distinguished experts say the jury's still out. Anyway, let's hope they're wrong—or we're all up shit's creek, huh? Keep the change."

Balding wheels squealed away, and she turned to face the rain, the building, the music, surprised at how pissed off she really, really was.

Lu liked the place. Very civil, she'd told her wryly a while back, very *Bardo,* very *Magic Mountain,* I mean très spiritual, Callie love, this Land of Just Enough Morphine. That day she'd managed a smile. Now, though, she was ashy and expressionless at a window, acknowledging no one. Jello and water untouched on a tray. Callie sat close by.

After a while the head turned with effort to face her. The eyes were still fully conscious Lu, though, trying to speak more clearly than the whispers.

"This is probably it."

"Uh-huh. You don't have to talk, love."

"Mmmm. It's gone, Cal. My sense of humor."

"Well, that's okay."

"Maybe not."

Lu was smaller than her now, she realized. Trying to describe to Pat the increasing physical devastation encountered each visit, the growing unrecognizability and continual subtle deforming of this once-powerful woman whom she'd loved as much as her life, words failed. She'd only been able to whimper, Well, it's interesting. Adding immediately, I mean, if that kind of thing interests you. And Pat, bless her, sensitive in a wordless way, had received both pain and sarcasm with a quiet, intelligent grace.

Today something else thumped inside Callie, in her throat and chest. There was a faint scent of vomit in the room, and she felt herself sweat suddenly, forcefully, caught up by a sheer nauseous wave of terror that almost sent her to the floor in a dead faint. Every once in a while it'd hit her like this, but today was the worst. When stuff in the room—plants and flowers, wall hangings, books and sheets and bottles of medicine—stopped reeling, she blinked away tears while her shirt clung wetly to panicked flesh. Her hands shook.

Lu ignored her. Then, after a few minutes, the head stopped bobbling, pain lines around mouth and eyes relaxed, and she sighed, leaned back almost comfortably in the armchair, and turned to face Callie with a calm, calm affection.

"Better, Cal. The drugs kicked in. Now we can talk."

"Huh," Callie croaked, "can you spare some for me?"

They shared a soundless laugh.

"Françoise called, Lu."

"Yes. I asked her to."

She had, it seemed, sent Françoise home to the kids late last night. With instructions that, if she was still alive by morning, Callie ought to visit.

First Callie found her ego blossoming at this news, and it killed her that, sick as she was, Lu could still touch her this way. She'd chosen to spend the time with *her* and not Françoise. Then other things occurred, unpleasantries: this was Françoise's mess more than hers. Why should she, Callie, be here on such precious time with that big clock in the sky tick-tick-tocking away? After all, it was another woman and her children Lu had opted for in the end.

What was it the bitch had said, at some gallery opening, the first time they'd met? *I find you very attractive.* Well, not surprising. Plenty of dykes thought that about Lu, but Françoise had had the gall to say it to her face, with Callie watching. And that was that—nine years down the drain. She'd seen the writing on that ever-crumbling wall of dyke monogamy quite clearly. Like most rotten things it was unfair, etcetera. She'd been left loveless, with half the earning power and more of the bills, having to salve Michael's confused anguish five days out of seven while Lu stepped easily into Françoise's dramatically more solvent life, continued career success, and a burgeoning circle of friends. What she'd never forgive Lu for was walking out on the kid, though, and into the arms of Françoise's conveniently waiting little brood. Then turning around and demanding weekend visits, making sure she kept a few talons in the flesh, making sure the boy still loved her. Rendering every Monday—the day after tearful return—some hot new hell. *Mom, Françoise's kids have a boat!*

Then, just a few months after meeting Pat, the ominous phone calls began, the news. Lu. Cancer. Which could gnaw up so many more unspoken lives than that of just its victims. They'd learn, over the months—all of Lu's families past and present would learn—to be humble in its presence. Watch it draw and quarter what they loved. Then watch it whip around unpredictably, crush their human quarrels and inflicted romantic cruelties and mutual bitternesses to less than squat beneath its deranged juggernaut hooves.

"I've already said good-bye to Françoise," Lu said, answering the unspoken. "But you and I, we've still got work to do."

"You're incorrigible, Lu. Says who?"

"Callie, it's me, your Lu. Your Lu. For a little while longer. Let's talk. Tell me things. How's Pat? Has she stopped making love to you yet?"

"Sometimes I really hate you, Lu."

"Hmmm." She nodded tiredly. "Listen, Callie, come with me. Come lie down with me for a while."

The place was set up perfectly for the frail and weak: short, bridgeable distances between surfaces to lean against, sit in, lie on, between armchairs and medicines and bed.

Flesh, Callie thought. How changeable it is. How easy to love or to shrink from.

Lu's strength was so completely, so astonishingly gone, ruined by what ate her insides, a creeping, awesome immensity of illness. A savage stalking disease in the face of which, Callie thought, you couldn't help but be afraid. You'd want to kneel down before it, supplicate, sob helplessly in an admiring sort of terror and fascination at its surefire, dauntless ability to strip so much away. Immortally replicating cells. They consumed, those cells—they were the ultimate consumers, in fact, giving nothing in return. Little demigods. Even so, they could not take everything. Lu's eyes were still warrior eyes, Callie saw, searching her face with embarrassing boldness and a shrewd, shrewd knowledge, as they lay side by side deep in pillows.

"So. Is it lesbian bed death, Callie? Not this—excuse the pun. Why don't you and Pat fuck anymore?"

"Is that any of your business?"

"I want you to be happy."

"Pretty late in the day for that, Lu—don't you think?" The words were out before she'd had a chance to stop them. Raw hands clutched her cheeks. Rage sparked out of the warrior eyes staring back at her with one last angry effort.

"Why don't you fight for what you want, Callie? I mean, you're always conceding defeat *before* the battle. It's as if you don't even desire victory. I've tried to save Michael from that."

Bitch, Callie thought, what else have you tried to save him from?

On the other hand, Lu was right.

"Maybe I'm afraid." She sighed. "Maybe fighting's not my way."

"Go to hell, love. You don't have that right. Fear's beside the point. You're a dyke, you have to fight. It's not a privilege—it's a duty."

That was the morning things changed between them again—the strangest morning of Callie's life, the last one of Lu's. Callie'd never fucked with her eyes before. But lying very close it was clear to her that eyes were what they had connecting them, and that was all they had. The pain was going to come back soon—maybe they were both afraid. Maybe that was why a strange bright willingness possessed them. It spun them up in the suffering arms of disease and of light; for a while made them just the same, no longer quite two people lying side by side on a bed, but one inseparable entity. The entity had no energy left to move or undress, only to see. Fully clothed, they put hands between each others' legs in a strange slow-motion kind of fever. Callie squirmed, white-hot sweating and afraid. This arousal, revulsion, terror, whatever, couldn't be physical, she thought. But it surely felt that way.

"Think of me loving you, Callie. Imagine me fucking you."

"Goddamn you, Lu."

"Imagine me fucking you. Hold on tight. But don't move. Don't come. Not yet."

Fuck you, Lu, Callie thought. You're the ultimate control freak. But the swell of something terrible started up at the core of her—wet, dangerous, waiting to explode.

"God, I hate you, Lu. I hate your fucking guts."

"Yes, Callie, that's good," she whispered, "say the truth. Then let me go."

"I mean, *fuck* you for having and leaving us. *Fuck* you for getting cancer. *Fuck* you and *fuck* you for dying. *Fuck* you for letting me go."

The hot, wet, dangerous swell went up her spine into her head, expanded in her throat and heart and cunt, and tingled down into her toes, but she didn't move, just swelled hot and bright with it, kept it inside, and she could feel her lover doing the same, could feel her feeling it too. Then the weight of deeds between them fell utterly away. For a flickering moment they were there without flesh, blood, or bone—inside something that was and was not them, but contained them like bottled essence of fireflies, burning. Callie rode the swell, struggled wildly when it almost escaped, kept it inside. She pressed against lost flesh, tired bones.

"There," Lu gasped. "Yes, there, like so."

They stayed that way, bright-lit, sweating, and breathless, waiting for some last searing, inevitable wave of the demigods' pain. It would pick one of them up this time with its awesome, superior strength—arrogantly, pitilessly. Flay her alive and take all away except a subtle fierce burning in the eyes. Then it would take that too with an unendurable scream, until whatever was left lay there withered and broken, a mass of suffering flesh. Until warrior heart stopped beating, and will and action ceased.

Before that, Lu managed one more thing. Leaning even closer, whispering into an ear, "Forgive me, love, for everything. But I just don't believe in endings." Then Callie pulled back from the pain and the light. And knowing, left her alone.

Michael practiced roller-blading all the next weekend under Pat's watching gaze. When a screw came loose they mended it together. Callie let them bond. Intermittently she was on the phone with Françoise, or family, or Arthur, or some of Lu's old friends, making memorial service arrangements. The boy came in to ask questions or to cry sometimes, and she held him.

Pat was quiet, doing things around the house. She busied herself with Michael mostly and let well enough alone. Callie noticed her for the first time in months: a womanish, boyish presence that might—just might—promise tenderness and delight.

"You've got a cute ass, Pat," she said that night, in their

room, "don't *you* drop dead on me any time soon."

"I wasn't planning to, honey."

"Prove it."

Half naked, Pat wheeled around enraged. Then grabbed her roughly, tears and warning in her eyes. "*You're* the one with something to prove tonight, lady. I mean, I know it's bad timing. But things are rough all over. Wake up, you! Wake up."

They rubbed each other into a frenzy on the bed, blessedly uninterrupted by the patter of little feet, and fell asleep naked. Hours later Callie woke to see Michael standing there in pajamas Lu'd given him, staring.

"You're naked."

"Uh-huh."

"Do you and Pat do sex?"

"Yes, Mike."

"Like Françoise and Mom Lu? I mean, yucchy kisses? When I grow up I'll have a wife. We'll make babies. I'll put my penis in her vagina."

"Yes, my love. And a lucky girl she'll be."

"I miss her," he said, and sobbed. She and Pat threw on robes, then cuddled him together until dawn. He finally slept.

"Yaaaah," Callie whispered. "Screw philosophy. Dying sucks."

"Or maybe," said Pat, "we just need to learn how."

The three of them rocked back and forth.

"Pat," she said, "lover, woman, who are you?"

"Not Lu, honey. But funny you should ask. I thought you never would." She smiled, half hero, half shadow in the dark. "Stick around some, doll—we will see."

*(1981-1994)*

Firebrand Books is an award-winning feminist and lesbian publishing house. We are committed to producing quality work in a wide variety of genres by ethnically and racially diverse authors. Now in our eleventh year, we have over eighty titles in print.

A free catalog is available on request from Firebrand Books, 141 The Commons, Ithaca, New York 14850, (607) 272-0000.